CHRISTMAS PROTECTION DETAIL

TERRI REED

LOVE INSPIRED SUSPENSE

INSPIRATIONAL ROMANCE

LOVE INSPIRED® SUSPENSE
INSPIRATIONAL ROMANCE

ISBN-13: 978-1-335-40322-3

Christmas Protection Detail

Copyright © 2020 by Terri Reed

Recycling programs for this product may not exist in your area.

This edition published by arrangement with Harlequin Books S.A.

For questions and comments about the quality of this book, please contact us at CustomerService@Harlequin.com.

Love Inspired
22 Adelaide St. West, 40th Floor
Toronto, Ontario M5H 4E3, Canada
www.Harlequin.com

Printed in U.S.A.

"Give me the baby."

"No." Nick backed away and curled protectively around the infant. "Stay back."

Kaitlyn edged between the man and Nick and the baby, aware of the barrel of the gun too close to her chest. Her heart thudded with fear, but she held her ground.

The wiry man let out a string of curses, turned and raced for the door.

Kaitlyn scooped up her weapon. "Stop where you are!"

The man paused at the door with his back to them.

"Drop your weapon and put your hands up!" Kaitlyn shouted, holding her weapon in a two-handed grip.

With a vicious curse, the man whirled around, his gun aimed at her head. His finger moved toward the trigger.

"No!" Nick shouted and shoved Kaitlyn out of the way with one hand while keeping Rosie tucked to his chest with the other.

The air whirled hot next to her ear as a bullet hit the monitor display...

Terri Reed's romance and romantic suspense novels have appeared on the *Publishers Weekly* top twenty-five and Nielsen BookScan top one hundred lists, and have been featured in *USA TODAY, Christian Fiction* magazine and *RT Book Reviews*. Her books have been finalists for the Romance Writers of America RITA® Award and the National Readers' Choice Award and finalists three times for the American Christian Fiction Writers Carol Award. Contact Terri at terrireed.com or PO Box 19555, Portland, OR 97224.

Books by Terri Reed

Love Inspired Suspense

Buried Mountain Secrets
Secret Mountain Hideout
Christmas Protection Detail

True Blue K-9 Unit: Brooklyn

Explosive Situation

True Blue K-9 Unit

Seeking the Truth

Military K-9 Unit

Tracking Danger
Mission to Protect

Visit the Author Profile page at Harlequin.com for more titles.

For God hath not given us the spirit of fear; but of power, and of love, and of a sound mind.

−2 Timothy 1:7

Thank you to my editors, Emily Rodmell and Tina James, as well as the whole team at Love Inspired Suspense. I appreciate you all and look forward to more stories together.

Thank you to my critique partner, Leah Vale, for not laughing when my dictation comes out like gobbledygook. You can decipher my thought process. A scary thing, that.

ONE

Deputy Kaitlyn Lanz climbed the short stepladder to reach the last few branches needing to be decorated on the Christmas tree in the Bristle Township Community Center. The combined celebration of the season and the retirement of Bristle Township's sheriff, James Ryder, was in full swing all around her. Christmas tunes played from the speakers mounted to the ceiling. The music competed with the many conversations taking place.

It seemed the whole town had turned out for the festivities. Kaitlyn had to admit she was pleased that so many people wanted to wish her boss—uh, former boss—well.

She sent up a quick prayer that nothing would mar the festive event. For some reason, she'd been anxious lately. Nothing specific, just a vague sense of doom that hit her at odd times. She chalked it up to losing the sheriff to fishing and traveling.

It had been several months since there'd been any real trouble in town or any need for the mounted patrol to mobilize. Not that she was complaining, because she loved being a part of the Bristle County sheriff's department's long tradition of patrols on horseback.

Like similar units in many Western states, the mounted patrol was comprised of both armed deputies and unarmed civilian volunteers, also referred to as auxiliary members. They provided search and rescue, as well as community and forest patrols. It was one of the various aspects of her job as keeper of the peace that utilized her many skills. She took pride in her job and always strove to do well at protecting the citizens of her town.

But tonight, she wasn't going to let anything keep her from enjoying the party.

"A little to the left."

The deep baritone voice caused her to jerk and fumble with the ornament she was attempting to hang on the large Douglas fir tree standing in the corner of the community center. Balanced on top of the stepladder to reach a high branch, she wobbled. So much for enjoying the party. Nick Delaney, the second in line to inherit the Delaney fortune, had become the bane of her existence over the past year.

He grasped her by the waist with surprising strength, stabilizing her on the short ladder. "Steady there."

She threw an irritated glance over her shoulder at the man. "I've got it."

"Of course. But maybe hang it a little to the left," he said, directing her placement of the glittery ornament.

Her heart thumped maddeningly. And not because she'd almost fallen from the ladder. Nick looked good tonight. As always. So maddening. Could he, just once, be unattractive?

He was dressed to impress in crisply creased black slacks and a finely tailored gray sport coat over a dark green mock turtleneck sweater. His dark hair was swept off his forehead to accentuate his chiseled cheekbones.

His dark eyes sparkled, and his grin was much too confident.

From the moment she'd met the younger son of the local eccentric billionaire, Nick's arrogance had rubbed her nerves raw.

Abruptly, she turned back to the tree, placed the ornament where she had intended and stepped down from the ladder, forcing him to release his hold and move back to give her room. "I like it where it is."

He shrugged. "You know best, Deputy."

She gritted her back teeth. He made the moniker sound pretentious. Turning her attention to the tree, she realized with a sinking sensation he'd been right. The turtledove glass bauble she'd brought from home needed to be a bit more to the left for symmetry.

Ah, well. She wasn't perfect and neither were her ornament hanging abilities. But she certainly wouldn't give Nick the satisfaction of knowing she regretted not listening to his advice. Had it been anyone else, she no doubt would have adjusted the ornament accordingly. What was it about Nick that put her on edge all the time?

She had a suspicion her irritation stemmed from the fact that he reminded her of her college boyfriend, Jason. A relationship that hadn't ended well.

"Here." Nick thrust a red box with a white bow at her.

She tucked her hands behind her back. She wasn't accepting a gift from the man. He'd no doubt think she owed him something in return. "You shouldn't have bought me a present."

Nick chuckled and his eyes danced with amusement. "I'm sorry to disappoint you, but it's for the tree." He opened the box to reveal a beautiful crystal angel figurine hanging from a white satin ribbon. "Everyone was asked to contribute an ornament, correct?"

Face heating from her obvious mistake, she nodded at the ornament. "Looks expensive."

He contemplated the figurine. "Probably. My mother liked expensive things."

From what Kaitlyn had gathered, Mrs. Delaney had passed away when Nick and his older brother, Ian, were teenagers. "Are you sure you want to hang it here? Shouldn't you hang it on the tree in your family home?"

"We haven't put up a tree," Nick said.

She couldn't remember a time when her family hadn't had a tree.

"Besides, Dad and Ian are in Ireland checking on our family holdings there and won't be back until the New Year."

A pang of sadness for him hit her unexpectedly. He'd be alone at Christmas in that big house. The Delaneys lived in a massive estate built on one of the mountaintops outside of town. She'd been to the palatial home during a case that had involved the elder Delaney and a buried treasure. Kaitlyn had never seen such luxury.

The Delaney family was a bit of an enigma to the rest of the inhabitants of Bristle Township. For the longest time they had kept to themselves, but then the treasure hunt had stirred up a great deal of dust for Kaitlyn's friend Maya Gallo-Trevino and her younger brother, Brady, putting them in danger.

It was also during this time that Kaitlyn had met Nick.

And since then it seemed like Nick's personal mission in life was to annoy her with his flirting and not-so-subtle hints that he'd like to date her.

She didn't date.

And even if she did, it wouldn't be with a man who had too much time and money on his hands and nothing to show for it. A man who no doubt thought he could buy his way out of anything.

"Does your father know you're offering this ornament up?" she asked.

Nick arched an eyebrow. "I don't need his permission. Besides, Dad and Ian expect me to represent the family at tonight's celebration. Here I am, doing my duty." He stepped past her to halt Brady Gallo. "Hi, Brady. Would you be willing to hang this on the tree for me?"

Brady broke out in a wide grin. "I can do it."

Kaitlyn's heart clenched. She loved Brady. In fact, the whole town did and was very protective of the young man with Down syndrome. Not sure Brady should be climbing onto the stepladder, Kaitlyn sent Nick a censuring glance. "I can do it."

Nick and Brady stared at her.

"I'll hold the ladder for you, Brady," Nick said with a censuring look of his own. "There's a space right up there next to the turtledove ornament."

Kaitlyn narrowed her gaze and pressed her lips together. The man was adept at getting under her skin.

Once Brady had the angel figurine securely hung, Nick helped him off the ladder and gave him a hug. "Good job, buddy."

Blinking in surprise, Kaitlyn echoed Nick's words. "Good job."

When Brady was out of earshot, Kaitlyn said, "I hadn't realized you two had become friends."

"He and Alex come to the house periodically to spar with me." Nick tweaked her braid. "Speaking of Alex, I think I'll go congratulate the new sheriff."

Flipping her braid over her shoulder, Kaitlyn stared in disbelief as he wove his way through the crowd toward her new boss. Spar with him? She had to admit the Delaneys did have a really nice dojo built on the lower floor of their home, but Kaitlyn hadn't known that Alex Trevino and Nick had become buddies. Why had Maya never mentioned it?

She watched as Nick congratulated Alex on becoming the county's new sheriff. Then Nick moved to Sheriff James Ryder to wish him well in his retirement.

She forced her thoughts away from the infuriating Nick Delaney, her stomach clenching with apprehension. Who would take Alex's place as a deputy?

It had to be someone with experience. The last thing the department needed was some yahoo thinking he or she understood small-town policing but then realizing the slow-paced yet complicated life in Bristle Township was anything but easy.

Kaitlyn let out a heavy sigh. She loved this town and its community. And she didn't have anything else in her life. Some would say she was married to the job, and she was okay with that, thank you very much.

No one needed to know about the trauma of her past or the invisible scars she carried. Her gaze strayed to Nick where he now stood at the refreshment table talking to the mayor. Especially not some wealthy man with an ego the size of the state of Colorado.

Nick Delaney stood off to the side of the refreshment table set up at one end of the community center's event room, sipping his sparkling apple cider. Garland entwined with twinkle lights hung from the walls and light fixtures.

Chairs and tables outfitted with cheery seasonal decorations dotted the huge space.

Outside, the steadily falling snow swirled on the frigid air, but inside was toasty warm. He tugged at the collar of his mock turtleneck. He was out of place among the residents of Bristle Township. Yet everyone had greeted him with warmth when he'd arrived an hour ago. Maybe he was finally finding a place to belong.

From where he stood, he had a perfect view of the Christmas tree and all the presents beneath for the big white elephant exchange that would be happening later. Nick had never attended such an exchange and wasn't quite sure what to make of the idea. The mayor had assured him he'd enjoy the tradition. One of many, it seemed. What a strange concept to have customs that went on from year to year. He'd lived a jet-set life. One year off to Rome. The next to Paris or Morocco. Nothing in his life was ever permanent.

However, with the help from the community church's pastor, he was learning to reform his self-indulgent ways. At first the idea of counseling had made Nick laugh, but then he'd decided he had nothing to lose other than a bunch of bad habits. What could it hurt?

Well, a lot, actually, but Nick was hopeful that dealing with the past would make the future as bright as the star at the top of the Christmas tree.

He'd grown fond of the welcoming community in the little Colorado town. Not something he'd ever expected when his eccentric father had moved into the county. Even his know-it-all, stick-in-the-mud brother, Ian, was becoming a pillar of the community.

Nick had resisted joining his father and brother, figuring the small mountain hamlet would just be boring and mundane. And he expected the citizens to be critical of the youngest son of the Delaney dynasty.

He'd been wrong. With the exception of a certain female deputy.

Nick's gaze traveled over the other partygoers, deep in their merriment, landing on said deputy. Kaitlyn Lanz. She wasn't dressed in her usual brown uniform. Tonight, she wore black slacks, black boots with low heels and a red sweater decorated with tiny light bulbs that flashed on and off. Her long blond curly hair had been corralled into a braid held by a big Christmas bow. A vision of loveliness.

He tracked Kaitlyn as she walked across the room toward the group of women preparing the cakewalk, apparently another of the town's traditions.

Fascinated with the length of Kaitlyn's neck, he found the graceful lines and strong jaw worthy of a master sculptor.

She was single and apparently not dating, or so her friend Leslie had shared with him. Kaitlyn, it seemed, hadn't dated since college. According to Leslie, no one really knew why.

He hoped maybe one day he would entice her to open up to him. But he knew that might happen when reindeer flew. Though around here it made more sense to wait for cows or horses to sprout wings, because that was the sort of livestock that occupied most of the ranches in this part of Colorado.

So far, every time he'd asked Kaitlyn for anything, whether it was for an actual date or for coffee, or even an opinion about the weather, she resisted.

He told himself he hadn't given up this past year because he liked the challenge. But who was he kidding?

He'd never liked a challenge. Except, apparently, when it came to Kaitlyn. Which was the oddest thing. He didn't quite know what to make of it. There was just something about the deputy that...

His cell phone vibrated in the front breast pocket of his sport coat. He plucked the device from the pocket, fully expecting to see either his father's or Ian's number. They would, no doubt, be checking to make sure he was attending the party, because they couldn't just trust him to do as he'd promised. Though, to be fair, they had reason.

Growing up, being shuffled back and forth between the family estate in Massachusetts and various boarding schools, or rather being kicked out of various boarding schools, had given his family reason to find him unreliable.

But he was trying to mend his ways.

He frowned at the number he didn't recognize. Had something happened to his father? His dad was in his eighties and had heart disease that required monitoring.

With dread gripping his chest and his mind a swirling mess of unease, he slid the button on the phone and answered, "This is Nick Delaney."

From the sounds coming at him through the device, Nick guessed someone was in a car or maybe a plane.

"Nick! Help me. I'm on my way to you. The roads in Bristle Township are so slick." A woman's voice, shaking with obvious fear, had the small hairs at the back of his neck rising. "I—"

Several loud, booming sounds echoed through the phone. Gunfire? Horror shuddered through Nick.

The woman let out a bloodcurdling scream.

The sickening sound of metal crunching against metal

reverberated into Nick's ear before the call dropped and only silence remained.

He stared at the device. What had just happened? Who had that been? Obviously, the woman knew him. But what did she mean she was on her way to him?

Whoever she was, this mysterious woman was in trouble. He had to help. He had to find Kaitlyn. She would know what to do. She couldn't refuse him this time.

From her place on the proverbial sidelines, back against the light and garland-festooned walls with a clear view of the exits, Kaitlyn watched her friends walking in a circle, waiting for the music to stop so they could vie for a spot on one of the large snowflake cutouts taped to the floor.

The point of the game was to be the last one standing on a snowflake in order to win one of the many donated cakes sitting on the nearby table. If Kaitlyn didn't need to watch every calorie, she'd want the lemon chiffon cake that Mrs. Johnson made every year.

Movement to her left caught her attention and she groaned beneath her breath. Nick Delaney was headed her way at a fast clip. He was a constant source of irritation, like a saddle sore. Despite the flare of attraction that continually caught her by surprise, she wasn't up to deflecting any more of his flirtations tonight. She had enough dealing with the coming change in the sheriff's department.

She didn't much like change. It caused chaos and stress.

On the verge of making a quick exit, she hesitated as she studied Nick's face. He didn't have his normal charming smile in place. Instead, obvious worry drew his dark eyebrows together and pinched in the sides of his well-shaped mouth. Her heart plummeted. Had something happened to his family?

He'd explained earlier that his brother and father were out of the country. She braced herself, not sure what he would expect her to do. Or was this some new ploy to coax her into a date?

A mix of dread and anticipation knotted her gut and kept her rooted in place. She really needed to figure out what it was about this man that threw her off balance. Normally, she was able to keep unwanted feelings in check. But not with him. Strange.

Without preamble, Nick said, "Kaitlyn, I need your help."

Her natural wariness flared. "Okay. With what?"

He held out his phone and stared at it. "I got the strangest call." His gaze lifted. The deep chocolate-brown orbs were cloudy with worry. "A woman is in trouble. She acted like she knew me and was on her way to me. She sounded scared, and I think she crashed her car."

Not what Kaitlyn had expected. "She's on her way to you? Meaning on her way here to Bristle Township?"

His shoulders lifted in a slight shrug. "Yes. She said something about the roads in town being slick." His troubled gaze bored into Kaitlyn. "I'm sure I heard gunfire before the car crashed. She's in trouble. We need to help her. I need *you* to help me help her."

Serving others was why she'd become a deputy. And she couldn't deny there was a bit of relief that, for once, Nick wanted her as a deputy.

Kaitlyn took the phone from him and searched for Hannah Nelson, the department's forensic and computer tech, among the party attendees. Hannah's long red hair was unmistakable. She was in the cakewalk. "This way."

With purpose lengthening her strides, Kaitlyn led the way to the edge of the cakewalk circle where Hannah was participating.

"What are we doing?" Nick asked.

Kaitlyn shot him a glance. He really was spooked. And it drove up her own anxiety. Kaitlyn called to her. "Hannah."

Hannah's green eyes darted to her. She waved.

Kaitlyn gestured for her to come over.

With a frown, Hannah stepped out of the circle and headed in their direction. "You just cost me a German chocolate cake."

"I'll make you one," Kaitlyn told her. "We need your expertise."

Hannah's gaze darted back and forth between Kaitlyn and Nick. A speculative gleam entered her eyes and a smile formed on her pink-glossed lips. "Really? With what?"

Kaitlyn ground her teeth together. Everyone in town knew that Nick had been flirting with her for nearly a year. And that she had been brushing him off. She held up the device. "I need you to find the location of the person who made the last call to Nick's phone. Someone is in trouble."

Hannah's expression sobered. "Of course. We should inform the sheriff."

"Agreed."

The trio hurried over to where the new sheriff, as well as the newly retired sheriff, stood surrounded by a group of well-wishers. Kaitlyn nudged her way forward through the crowd.

Sheriff Ryder's bushy gray eyebrows rose to his hairline. "Is there something you wanted?"

Her gaze bounced between the two men. She wasn't sure which one she should address. Then Sheriff Ryder's index finger came up and pointed at Alex.

Sheriff Ryder was always so adept at reading her. Kaitlyn focused her attention on Alex. "We have a potential crash victim. Nick received a phone call from a mysterious woman. He heard what sounded like gunfire and a crash. Apparently the woman is on her way here. But we don't know where she is exactly. I want permission to have Hannah ping her phone."

Alex nodded. "Of course. Keep me apprised of the situation."

"Yes, sir." Kaitlyn retreated to where Nick and Hannah waited. "Let's go."

They hurried to put on coats and head out into the snowy December night. The community center was attached to the Bristle Township Community Christian Church, which sat at one end of town. They hustled along the sidewalk and Kaitlyn was thankful for the dusting of rock salt so that none of them slipped in their haste to get to the station.

Rather than entering through the front door, they went around to the back, where Hannah's newly reconstructed lab was located.

When a group of treasure hunters had torched the building, the Delaney family had paid to have the department rebuilt and equipped with all the high-tech equipment possible for the deputies and the forensic lab.

Hannah didn't even take off her coat. She went straight to her workstation to plug Nick's phone into her computer and got to work. Within seconds, she said, "The call pinged off the tower at the top of Delaney Hill." A moniker the locals had recently taken to calling the mountain where the Delaneys had built their home. "She must be somewhere on the road up to the estate."

Nick grabbed his phone and unplugged it from her computer. "Thank you."

He rushed toward the exit.

Kaitlyn raced after him and grabbed his arm. "Hey, what do you think you're doing?"

"I'm going to find her." He shrugged off her hand. "She needs help."

"You're a civilian. Somebody trained to provide help needs to go."

He flashed her one of his smiles, but it didn't dispel the anxiety in his eyes. "Then we can go together. I'll even let you drive."

"You'll let me…?" She rolled her eyes.

Digging his keys from his coat pocket, he held them out to her. "You can drive my Humvee. It's better equipped than yours."

Much as she wanted to argue that point, she didn't. Because he was right. The big square vehicle he drove was state-of-the-art with armor plating and shatterproof windows and was built to navigate the terrain. It seemed everything that the Delaneys owned was state-of-the-art.

"Fine." She plucked the keys from his hand and turned to Hannah. "Can you inform the sheriff? And if for some reason that phone moves, let me know."

"You got it," Hannah promised.

"Come with me," Kaitlyn said to Nick. Instead of immediately going out the door, Kaitlyn stopped where the department's tactical gear was stored. She grabbed a duty belt and two flak vests. She tossed one to Nick. "Put that on."

He stared at her for a moment. "You believe that I heard gunfire?"

Why would he think she wouldn't? "Better to be prepared than dead."

He gave a sharp nod of his head and slipped the vest on. "Wow, I had no idea how heavy these things were."

She didn't mention the weight of the utility belt strapped around her hips. Velcroing her vest in place over her Christmas sweater, she grabbed her department-issued shearling jacket and put it on, covering her sweater, which thankfully had an off switch to kill the blinking lights. "Let's roll."

Once they were settled in the large SUV, Kaitlyn fired up the engine and drove through town. She had to admit the ride was smooth. Within moments, she turned onto the long winding road that led up the second-tallest mountain in the county. The bright headlights of the SUV cut through the darkness and bounced off the snow. They'd reached the summit near the gate of the estate when the SUV's headlights swung across the accident scene. A dark gray sedan with chains on the tires had slid off the road into a tree.

Nearby, a black SUV was parked at an angle and two men were dragging a female from the sedan's driver's seat. Kaitlyn's hands gripped the steering wheel as she brought the vehicle to an abrupt halt.

Nick popped open his door and slid out.

"Wait!" Kaitlyn yelled at him. The fine hairs at her nape quivered.

He froze, standing with the door open. "Kaitlyn?"

Were these men Good Samaritans? Or something far more sinister?

The men let go of the woman, letting her flop into

the snow. Then both men swiveled to aim high-powered handguns at them.

"Take cover!" Kaitlyn reached for the duty weapon at her side. She'd wanted Nick to appreciate her for the capable deputy she was, but not at the risk of his life.

TWO

A barrage of gunfire hit Nick's SUV and echoed through his ears. He dived back onto the passenger seat. The glass separating him from the incoming bullets shuddered, and little divots pockmarked the outer layer. The energy of the projectiles dispersed outward into spiderweb-like fractures, but the window held against the onslaught. He was thankful for the bulletproof protection his father had insisted on.

With gun in hand, Kaitlyn popped open her door. "Call for backup."

Fear that she'd be hit speared Nick. "Kait, stay inside!"

"I'm not letting these two bozos get the better of me." Wedging her weapon between the door and the vehicle, she shouted, "Sheriff's department. Put down your weapons."

Instead of complying, the men shot at her, and she returned fire, causing the two armed men to duck behind their vehicle. Kaitlyn's bullets pierced the metal of the other utility vehicle, unlike Nick's armored SUV.

He hadn't realized she had a competitive streak. Or maybe it was just that she was out for blood after seeing somebody helpless being hurt. His heart pumped as he remembered how the men had so callously dropped the woman when they realized he and Kaitlyn had driven up. He could not abide those who preyed on the weak.

Nick activated the SUV's Bluetooth. "Call Alex Trevino."

Within a second Alex was on the line. "Nick?"

"We're being shot at! Near the summit. And we need an ambulance."

"We're on our way," Alex promised.

Kaitlyn reloaded her weapon, giving the two men time to jump into their SUV. The taillights glowed bright red before the backup lights came on. The vehicle reversed away from the crash site and toward where Kaitlyn had brought Nick's SUV to a halt.

Anticipating the other SUV was going to ram into them, Nick braced himself. "Kaitlyn! Move."

She jumped out of the way, rolling on the ground and coming up firing at the SUV. The impact of the other vehicle ramming its back end into the front end of Nick's SUV jarred through Nick with a violent shudder. Kaitlyn continued to fire at the vehicle as it sped away, taking out its back window. Soon the red taillights were a distant glow swallowed by the darkness of the mountain.

Nick scrambled out of the SUV and rushed to the aid of the mysterious woman lying on the cold ground, dark hair splayed in the white snow illuminated by the headlights of his SUV. Blood seeped into the snow from a wound on her head. He knelt down next to her and checked for a pulse.

He breathed a sigh of relief to feel the faint beat against his fingers. "She's alive."

He brushed hair away from the woman's face. Recognition tore through him. He sat back on his heels. "Lexi?"

Kaitlyn dropped down next to him. "You know this woman?"

"Yes. I do. Her name is Lexi Eng." What was Lexi doing in Bristle Township? How had she found him? And why were men with guns trying to take her?

Kaitlyn gently shook the woman. "Lexi, can you hear me?"

Lexi's eyes fluttered open. She groaned and shifted.

"Don't move," Kaitlyn said. "An ambulance is on its way."

Lexi's onyx-colored gaze met Nick's. Her eyes widened and a small *oh* formed on her red lips. "Nick," she said, her voice barely above a whisper.

"You're okay. We aren't going to let anything happen to you," Nick assured her. Where was that ambulance?

"You said if I ever needed you…" Lexi grew agitated. Kaitlyn kept her from sitting up, so Lexi grabbed for the front of his shirt. "Oh, no. Nick, you have to keep her safe. Promise me."

"Uh, sure." He wasn't sure who *her* referred to, but the desperate look in Lexi's gaze clutched at his heart.

Lexi slumped back. "Good." Her face twisted with pain and she cried out before her body went limp and her eyes rolled back.

"Lexi!"

Kaitlyn checked her pulse. "She passed out. She may be bleeding internally."

"How can you tell?"

"I've seen injuries like this before," Kaitlyn said.

Agitated with the need to fix this, he asked, "What can I do to help her?"

"Pray the ambulance arrives soon."

Nick sank back on his heels. That he could do. He sent up a silent plea. He thought about what Lexi had asked of him. "Keep who safe?"

Not many people asked him for anything beyond his name, money and influence. Without those things, he could disappear and no one would notice.

Distant sirens heralded the imminent arrival of help. Hope filled his chest.

Kaitlyn stood and kicked one of the back tires of the sedan Lexi was driving. "There's a bullet hole here. Probably why she crashed."

A noise, strange and out of place, filled the interior of the car. The sound reminded Nick of his nana's calico when the feline caught its tail in the door. Nick jumped to his feet with a sudden jolt of adrenaline. Kaitlyn drew her weapon as she cautiously opened the back passenger door.

She quickly holstered her weapon. "Nick, there's a baby here."

"What?" Nick nudged Kaitlyn aside to confirm for himself.

There was, indeed, an infant strapped in a car seat covered with a fuzzy pink blanket. The little girl had a full head of dark hair. She was bundled up, so it was hard to tell her age. Not that Nick would have been able to judge correctly. The closest he'd ever come to children were the ones he saw at church on Sundays.

Concern arced through him. Though he'd never held an infant before, the urge to do something prompted him to reach for the baby.

"No," Kaitlyn warned. "Wait for the paramedics to arrive. If the baby's hurt, we don't want to injure her more."

Thankful for her clearheadedness, he nodded and stepped back. He'd been so focused on Lexi he hadn't noticed the pink floral diaper bag lying a few feet away. A few diapers, a couple of pieces of baby-sized clothing and a bottle were strewn about the ground.

From inside the car, the baby's gurgling cries turned into full-fledged, lung-filled wailing. No doubt the little one was scared and wanting her mother. Empathy twisted in Nick's chest and he fisted his hands to keep from trying to comfort the baby.

He glanced at Lexi. Was she the child's mother?

Or had she kidnapped this child?

The thought filled him with unease and dread.

No. He rejected that idea. If those men had been after Lexi because of the baby, they would've taken the infant. There was something else going on here and he was determined to get to the bottom of it.

The ambulance rolled up, followed closely by Sheriff Trevino's vehicle. The siren abruptly cut off, leaving the world with only the sound of the baby's cries from within the sedan.

Kaitlyn rushed to the medics. "Unconscious woman with unknown injuries. There's a baby in the back seat. We didn't move her."

Alex halted beside Kaitlyn. While she told him the situation, Nick moved out of the way. He hated the helplessness seeping through him as the two paramedics tended to Lexi and the child. Money and influence couldn't fix Lexi's injuries, but Nick would use all his resources to protect her child. Assuming she was Lexi's.

After giving Alex her verbal report, Kaitlyn took out her phone and started taking pictures. The tire tracks in the snow, the crashed car and the bullet hole in the tire.

The female paramedic removed the car seat from the back of the sedan and handed the infant to Nick. "Hold on to her."

He was surprised by the weight of the child and car seat in his hands. And even more disconcerted by the weight of responsibility descending heavily on his shoulders.

Keep her safe, Lexi had said. Obviously Lexi had loved this child. He made a silent promise to Lexi and God that he would do whatever he could to make sure this infant was taken care of.

After loading Lexi into the ambulance, the female paramedic came back to Nick and put out her hands, clearly expecting him to hand the infant over.

He shook his head. "I'm coming with you and the baby."

"Nick."

Kaitlyn's voice drew his attention. She shook her head.

"Yes," he said. "I'm staying with the child."

Just then another SUV rolled up. Deputies Daniel Rawlings and Chase Fredrick stepped out of the vehicle. Nick nodded at the two men as he passed them to enter the back bay of the ambulance. "Kaitlyn will fill you in. I'm going to the hospital with them."

Kaitlyn rushed forward. "Nick, you don't have to go. I will stay with the victims."

"Her name is Lexi. And the baby's my responsibility now. At least until you find Lexi's family."

"You don't need to," she said. "I'll keep them safe."

"Lexi asked me to." No one ever asked much of him. He would do the right thing and honor her request. He climbed into the back of the ambulance with the female attendant, who immediately started an IV in Lexi's arm.

Shaking her head, Kaitlyn joined him and slammed the door shut.

The ambulance engine fired up.

"Hang on," the paramedic said.

Nick braced his feet apart and wedged the baby carrier between his ankles. Kaitlyn's steady stare was unnerving, as if she were trying to see inside his head. But he was good at keeping up the wall. He gave her an impertinent grin. As expected, she frowned and jerked her gaze away.

A prick of guilt stung Nick. He shouldn't use his tricks on Kaitlyn, but ingrained habits were hard to break. He dropped his gaze to the child at his feet. The paramedic had given the baby a pacifier, and she sucked happily on it. Big dark eyes stared up at him. So trusting. So innocent.

A strange warmth spread through his chest. He didn't understand the sensation. He tugged at the collar of his mock turtleneck.

"How do you know this woman? Did you date her?"

Kaitlyn's sharp tone grated on his nerves even as his conscience reminded him he deserved her censure for deliberately annoying her.

"No. We were friends." He didn't date. Dating implied emotional connections. The thought of lowering his guard and exposing his inner thoughts and feelings made him itchy. Despite his reputation, he kept himself isolated when not in public.

Yet the only woman he'd ever considered actually dating, as in getting to know and opening up to, was Kaitlyn. There was something about her that piqued more than just his interest in her as a beautiful woman. She had depths that called to him. And the fact that she wasn't impressed with his family name or wealth was unique.

That she wasn't impressed with him made her very captivating. What would it take to impress her? What would it take to make her see him as someone worthy of knowing?

Pastor Brown had commented that maybe he pursued Kaitlyn because there was no chance she'd say yes. But Nick wasn't looking for a fling. He was looking for... He honestly didn't know. The concept of commitment was so foreign, yet still intriguing.

"Why was she here in Bristle Township?"

Nick met Kaitlyn's gaze. "I have no idea. You know as much as I do at this point."

Though Kaitlyn's eyes held doubt, she fell silent as the ambulance raced for Bristle Township Hospital. When they arrived, Nick and Kaitlyn disembarked from the ambulance and moved out of the way so that the paramedics could remove Lexi and wheel her inside the hospital.

Nick hustled forward, carrying the car seat with the baby tucked inside. As they walked through the doors, the paramedic held up a hand. "Wait here. Someone will come out to get her."

At that moment, the baby spit out her pacifier and started crying again, her little arms flailing and dislodging the blanket tucked around her tiny body.

"Shhhh. Little one. It's okay," Nick crooned, unsure if he was doing any good. He looked at Kaitlyn for help.

She held up her hands. "Don't ask me. I don't know anything about babies. I need to talk to hospital security." She strode away.

With a sigh, Nick headed for the waiting area. He

settled on a seat where he could keep an eye on Kaitlyn where she stood talking to hospital security near the entrance. Did she believe the gunmen would come to the hospital to finish what they'd started?

Anxiety twisted in his gut. He gently pressed the pacifier to the baby's mouth. "Come on, sweetie. Take this thing."

Using her tongue, the little girl pushed the pacifier out.

He had no idea what to do as the baby wailed. He'd never been confronted with a situation like this one before. Give him a boat to steer, a plane to pilot or a race car to drive and he was confident. But a child who wouldn't stop crying? Beyond his expertise.

"You're safe now, sweetie." And he didn't even know the baby's name. "I've got you."

An older couple sat nearby. The woman smiled at Nick. "She might need a diaper change."

Nick winced. There was an odorous stench coming from the baby, but he didn't know how to change a diaper. Nor did he have one with him. He thought about the diaper bag he'd seen near Lexi's car. He quickly got out his phone and texted Alex, asking him to grab the bag and all the baby stuff.

But he still needed to figure out what to do now for the baby.

Cradling the car seat in his arms, he went up to the counter where the intake nurse sat. The midtwenties brunette glanced up at him. "Can I help you?"

"Yes, you can." He glanced at her name badge. "Doris." He gave her one of his most charming smiles. "This little one needs some attention. I was told a doctor would be examining her. Can you make that happen for me? I could so use your help."

The woman's cheeks pinkened. "I'll see what I can do, Mr. Delaney."

Not surprised the woman was aware of who he was, Nick said, "I'd appreciate that, Doris."

He moved back to the waiting area and off to the far side, away from everyone else, trying not to disturb them with the baby's cries or smell.

The older woman who had talked to him earlier waved, gaining his attention. "Rock her," she instructed and set her bent arms in a swaying motion.

Deciding it was good advice, he threaded the baby carrier over his forearms then began to rock back and forth. The baby's cries settled to hiccups.

Eventually, a nurse came out and walked over. "We're ready for the baby now."

"I'm coming with you," he said.

The nurse hesitated. "Are you the father?"

"I'm responsible for her."

"You're her legal guardian, then?"

Nick swallowed, then smiled, pouring on as much charm as he could muster while anxiety chomped through his gut. "The baby's mother asked me to watch her. I wouldn't want to disappoint Lexi when she wakes up."

"Nick." Kaitlyn stepped to his side. "Let the nurse do her job. The baby will be in good hands. We need to talk."

With a nod of thanks to Kaitlyn, the nurse carried the baby away.

Nick ran a hand through his hair as he faced Kaitlyn. She wasn't alone. Nick hadn't noticed that Alex, holding the pink flowered diaper bag, and Deputy Daniel Rawlings had arrived at the hospital.

"Did you catch the men who hurt Lexi?" Nick asked.

"Not yet," Alex said. He set the bag down. "But we will. I've alerted the state patrol in case they've headed out of the county."

Nick could only hope the men who'd caused Lexi's crash would give up and disappear, but he didn't think that would happen. If only he had a clue why Lexi had sought him out. What could have brought her to Bristle Township and his doorstep?

"Tell us about Lexi Eng," Kaitlyn said, as a hot stab of something unfamiliar jabbed at her. Jealousy? Really? She shook it off.

Now was not the time to be distracted by irrational emotions. She needed to stay focused. Zero in on the issue of the woman in the car and the men targeting her. Nick admitted to knowing this woman and she'd been on her way to find him. Kaitlyn needed to understand why.

And she didn't want to examine her own motives in uncovering the truth. It was enough the woman had been hunted and hurt by bad men. Kaitlyn couldn't abide evil in any form. She'd make sure they were brought to justice.

Nick's gaze bounced between her and the new sheriff and Daniel. "I met Lexi about three years ago in New York. She is—was—a graphic designer when I knew her. We met at a charity function and became friends."

Right. Friends. Kaitlyn wrestled with that unfamiliar sensation again. It twisted in her stomach and constricted her chest. No, she couldn't be jealous. She wouldn't let herself be. It was only anxiety that made her heart race and her jaw tight. And she decided she was anxious because this woman had brought danger to their community. Whatever she'd been involved in had resulted in disaster.

"You kept in touch?" Alex asked.

"No. I left New York, and last I heard, she'd taken a job in Washington, DC," Nick replied. "I have no idea how she tracked me down."

Kaitlyn's eyebrows twitched. A whirlwind romance. A fling with no commitments. So typical. Exactly the reason she'd been avoiding all his invitations. She didn't want to be another one of his conquests. Even hearing through the town grapevine that Nick was apparently in counseling with Pastor Brown didn't help Kaitlyn trust Nick.

"Why is she seeking you out now?" Kaitlyn asked. "And with a baby in tow?"

"I don't know." His perplexed expression appeared genuine. "Your guess is as good as mine."

A knot formed in her stomach. "Is the baby yours?"

He drew back. "What? No! I haven't seen Lexi in three years."

She was unsure she believed him, and her only response was "Hmm."

His jaw firmed. "I'm telling you the truth."

"We'll have to wait for Lexi to wake up and tell us." She focused on Alex. "Should I call the state child protective services?"

"We'll hold off until we have the woman's prognosis," Alex said. "We'll have to make arrangements for childcare until Ms. Eng can care for her baby again."

"Hey, wait a second." Nick took a step forward, asserting himself and forcing Kaitlyn to face him. "Lexi asked me to keep the baby safe. You heard her say the words. The little one will stay with me."

Kaitlyn stared at him. She didn't understand him. Caring for a baby would be hard work and a big responsibility. And certainly wouldn't be in his wheelhouse. He couldn't care for a child. "No way—" A strong hand on her shoulder prevented her from saying more. She looked at her new boss.

"We'll keep the mother's wishes in mind," Alex said. "But for now, all we can do is wait and pray Ms. Eng recovers."

Nick paced the waiting area. What was taking so long? Why hadn't the nurse returned with the baby? Was there something wrong with her? His stomach flipped. Had she been injured in the crash or worse?

Nervous energy coursed through his veins. And what about Lexi? Someone had run her off the road and then attempted to kidnap her. How extensive were her injuries? What could he do to help?

The only thing he could think of was to hire security for her. His father always used a personal protection agency out of Boston. As soon as Nick had a moment, he would contact Trent Associates and have them send a team to keep Lexi and her baby safe.

"You're really upset," Kaitlyn commented.

He paused, taking in the puzzled way she stared at him. "Of course I am. I'm not trained like you to take trauma in so casually."

Her eyebrows jumped. She opened her mouth, then clamped her lips together.

Before he could consider what she might have intended to say, the emergency room doors opened and the nurse returned, carrying the car seat over one arm and the baby in the other, the little girl now happily sucking on her pacifier.

Nick rushed forward, surprised by the amount of relief that flooded him at the sight of the child. "Is she okay?"

"She's a healthy three-month-old and such a sweetie," the nurse said. "We gave her a bottle and changed her diaper."

Nick reached for the little girl.

The nurse held on tight and looked at Alex. "Sheriff?"

Alex gave a nod. "She'll be fine with Mr. Delaney."

Relinquishing her hold, the nurse gingerly put the baby into Nick's arms. So tiny. Vulnerable. He'd never held an infant before and was afraid he'd drop her. But he couldn't let anyone, especially Kaitlyn, see his insecurity.

"She should be seen by a pediatrician soon," the nurse instructed.

"I'll see to it," Nick promised.

Over the nurse's shoulder he met Kaitlyn's frown. Clearly, she didn't think he was capable of taking care of this child. He wasn't surprised by her skepticism. But he was sure going to do his best.

"Any news on Ms. Eng?" Alex asked the nurse.

"I can check for you." The nurse hurried away.

Now that the baby was quiet and peaceful, Nick moved over to the bank of chairs by the window.

Carefully, he put the baby back in her seat and tucked the blanket around her, noticing the monogrammed name in the corner. Rosie.

The perfect name for a perfect little girl. He smoothed back her thick dark hair and stared into her big dark eyes as she made sucking noises on the pacifier. "Don't worry, Rosie. I'll protect you."

The only thing he'd ever been tasked with protecting before was his family's good name. An intangible thing, really. And something he'd rebelled against. But this sweet baby girl… Every cell in his body screamed with the need to keep her safe.

When a doctor in green scrubs walked out with a grim expression on his face, dread gripped Nick's gut. Sitting frozen with the baby at his feet, he watched as the doctor talked to the sheriff and Kaitlyn. The doctor shook hands with Alex and then walked back through the double doors.

Nick stood, his gaze locking with Kaitlyn's. The troubled look in her eyes didn't bode well.

She walked over to him. "Lexi's in a coma. The doctor isn't sure she'll wake up. She had severe internal bleeding and trauma."

Sorrow pinched his heart. "Poor Lexi. I want to take Rosie to her."

"Rosie?"

He showed her the monogrammed blanket.

"Ah."

"I know Lexi is unconscious, but having her baby close might help," he pressed, determined to make Kaitlyn see his logic.

For a moment, she didn't respond. Then she nodded. "It couldn't hurt. Come with me."

After clearing a visit to Lexi's room with the sheriff, Nick carried the baby in his arms to a room where Lexi lay comatose. She had a breathing tube, and machines monitored her vitals.

Seeing the once vibrant woman like this sent a jolt of shock through Nick. He steadied himself and held the baby next to Lexi. The baby turned her face toward her mother as if breathing in her scent. Nick's heart pounded with tenderness and sorrow. He lifted a prayer heavenward for Lexi.

The hospital room door slammed open. Shock jolted through Nick as two men wearing lab coats burst into the room with weapons drawn. The same two men who'd caused Lexi's crash.

THREE

Kaitlyn's heart jumped in her throat. Reacting on instinct and training, she withdrew her sidearm to meet the threat coming through the door. The same two men who'd been at the crash site now held them at gunpoint. Somehow these men had managed to slip past the hospital security and found white doctor's coats so they could pose as medical personnel and gain access to badges that would allow them into restricted areas.

"Deputy, drop your weapon," one of the men said.

He had sandy hair and cold blue eyes that sent a shiver down Kaitlyn's spine. She ground her molars together. No way did she want to give up her sidearm, but she was outnumbered. She pushed back the prickling of fear. There had to be a way to alert the sheriff.

Hoping to buy time, she slowly lowered her weapon to the floor, her gaze catching on the cord attached to the oxygen monitor clipped to Lexi's index finger. Kaitlyn shifted her position to better reach the cord. As she rose, she subtly yanked on the cord, pulling it from Lexi's finger.

Knowing there would be a twenty-second delay before

an alarm sounded, Kaitlyn stepped in front of Nick and the baby. She prayed this didn't get her killed.

Right on time, a shrill beeping from the monitor display pierced the room. Rosie let out a protesting wail. Kaitlyn couldn't blame the infant. The noise was ear-splitting.

"What did you do? You'll pay for this!" the blond gunman shouted with malice twisting his face. "We have to go!" He yanked open the door and ran out.

The other man rushed forward, his gaze on Lexi. Was that concern or fear in his eyes? "Is she okay?"

"Thanks to you, she's in a coma," Kaitlyn replied. "What are you after?"

The wiry man pointed his Glock at Nick. "Give me the baby."

"No." Nick backed away and curled protectively around the infant. "Stay back."

Kaitlyn edged between the man and Nick and the baby, aware of the barrel of the gun too close to her chest. Even with a flak vest on, being shot at such a close range would cause damage. A broken rib, bruising and pain. Her heart thudded with fear, but she held her ground.

The wiry man let out a string of curses, turned and raced for the door.

Kaitlyn scooped up her weapon. "Stop where you are!"

The man paused at the door with his back to them.

"Drop your weapon and put your hands up!" Kaitlyn shouted, holding her weapon in a two-handed grip and hoping the tremors racking her body didn't show.

With a vicious curse, the man whirled around, his gun aimed at her head. His finger moved toward the trigger.

"No!" Nick shouted and shoved Kaitlyn out of the

way with one hand while keeping Rosie tucked to his chest with the other.

Kaitlyn stumbled to the side in stunned surprise just as the man fired, the loud bang echoing off the walls. The air whirled hot next to her ear as the bullet hit the monitor display.

Regaining her balance, Kaitlyn raised her firearm, but the gunman slipped out the door and escaped.

She raced after him. "Stop!"

At the end of the hallway, a hospital security guard rounded the corner, colliding with the gunman. They grappled for the gun. Kaitlyn ran toward the men. A loud bang filled the hallway, pounding at her ears.

The gunman dropped to the floor.

The security guard, a local named Henry Drummond, backed away, shock on his face. "I didn't mean to. It was an accident. He wouldn't let go of the gun."

Though the words were muffled by the ringing in her ears, she said to Henry, "This is not your fault. You did your job."

Slowing, Kaitlyn approached the downed man, kicking the gun that had fallen from his hand to the side before squatting to check for a pulse. There was none.

The sound of pounding feet bounced off the wall. She looked up to see Alex and Daniel running toward her.

"Kaitlyn?" Alex skidded to a halt and put his hand on her shoulder. "Are you hit?"

"No." She rose and shook her head. "He's gone. But there was another one. He has on a lab coat with an access badge." She explained what had happened and gave a detailed description of the attacker.

"We have to find the other gunman before he leaves the hospital." Addressing Henry, Alex said, "Go to the video monitoring room. See if you can locate him on the security feed. Then radio me, but stay put."

Henry shook himself and seemed to come out of the stunned stupor he had retreated to. "Yes, sir." He took off, talking into his radio.

A moment later a Code Silver announcement came over the PA system, the code to alert the hospital staff to an active shooter.

To Daniel, Alex said, "Do a room-by-room search. And be careful."

Daniel nodded and started the arduous job of hunting for the second gunman.

"Should I go with him?" Kaitlyn asked, itching to find the man who'd burst into the room and threatened them all.

"No," Alex said. "I need you here, protecting our victim."

"Yes, sir." Kaitlyn hurried back to Lexi's now quiet room. A nurse checked the comatose woman's vitals. But it was Rosie and Nick who had Kaitlyn gaping. The little girl had fallen asleep in Nick's arms.

"You saved our lives," Nick said, his deep voice tinged with awe.

Uncomfortable with his praise, she said, "You saved mine. If you hadn't pushed me when you did, I'd be dead."

His dark-eyed gaze held hers. "I did what anyone would do. But you were the brave one."

Her chest tightened. She'd been scared. A fact she didn't want to dwell on, so she focused on the infant. "I'm surprised she's sleeping."

With a quiet chuckle, Nick said, "Me, too. She has to be exhausted. I know I am."

The sheriff returned a few moments later. "The guy's nowhere to be found. Daniel and Chase, when he arrives from the crash site, will provide security for Lexi."

"What about the baby?" Nick asked.

Alex sighed. "I called the state child protective services. They can't send someone until early next week, so we'll have to find somewhere safe for the child in the meantime."

Kaitlyn mentally filtered through the various people in town she thought might take the baby and keep her safe. She kept coming back to her own parents.

They loved children. Her mom had been hinting they wanted grandchildren. Not something that would happen anytime soon in Kaitlyn's future. Having children would require having a relationship, and she couldn't go there. After her experience in college with a narcissistic ex-boyfriend who'd cost her not only a job she loved but her peace of mind, as well, she wasn't sure she could allow anyone close again. She wasn't willing to put her trust or her heart at risk. The last time had left her feeling helpless and unsure of herself. And she'd vowed never again.

But she was strong, powerful now, and she would not let the past define her. She didn't need to live up to anyone else's expectations. Only her own.

"I'm sure my parents would take her in, and I can stay with them to provide protection," she said.

"She'll stay with me, of course," Nick said at the same time.

Kaitlyn's gaze jumped to him.

"I am going to take care of this baby. I promised Lexi," he insisted.

What was going through his mind? "You don't have to do this. Just because the woman sought you out does not make her or her child your responsibility." Unless he *was* the baby's daddy. What did Kaitlyn really know about Nick Delaney?

He looked her in the eye. "I made a promise."

The determination etched on his handsome face was confusing and yet stirred something uncomfortable inside of her that she didn't want to examine. She doubted Nick knew anything about children, let alone possessed the knowledge of how to care full-time for a three-month-old baby. "You'll be in way over your head. It's better if we seek help elsewhere."

Rosie began to fuss in Nick's arms. A fleeting look of panic entered his eyes. Kaitlyn arched an eyebrow. He rocked the child, and soon the fussing turned to gurgling hiccups as she settled back to sleep.

The sight of Nick holding the baby did funny things to Kaitlyn's insides. What was that about?

She was not going soft on this man.

Nick looked at her with defiance in his eyes. "See? I know what to do. She needs some love and care." He turned to Alex. "Besides, the estate is a fortress. Anyone would be foolish to think they could breach our security."

Though Kaitlyn agreed the Delaney estate had the most elaborate security system she'd ever encountered, she still had her doubts. "What happens when the baby cries through the night? Or when she needs to eat or have her diaper changed? Are you really up for the task of parenting this baby, even for a short time?"

His dark eyes hardened. "I know you don't believe in me, Kaitlyn. But I can do this. I will do this."

Before she could come up with an appropriate response, Alex interjected. "Nick, thank you for the offer. We'll take you up on it. For tonight, at the very least."

Kaitlyn stared at her boss. "Are you sure?"

"We don't know who is after them or why the baby and her mother are in danger. Their protection is our priority. The Delaney estate is the best choice. And you will stay with them, Kaitlyn."

"Me?" A deep panic reared inside of her. Alex was sending her, alone, with Nick and the baby? No. No, no, no. "Couldn't Daniel…?"

Alex held up his hand, his expression hardening. "Kaitlyn, I need you to do this."

She'd never heard Alex use such a firm tone or seen him so fierce. It was a bit intimidating. But he would need to be fierce to be the sheriff of Bristle Township. He had big shoes to fill. So she resolved that she would do as her new boss asked, no matter how unsettled she was by the idea of being in close proximity to Nick for any length of time. "Yes, sir."

Alex nodded his thanks. "In the morning we can deal with making other arrangements if necessary. I'll need you to write up your incident report and then take Nick and the baby home."

Expecting to see a smirk on Nick's face for getting his way, she was unnerved by the tenderness in his eyes as he strapped Rosie into the carrier. Kaitlyn hated to admit to the kernels of respect and admiration for his determination to protect the little girl germinating inside of her.

He was too handsome and charming for her to take him seriously. Yet he seemed sincere. She wondered how long it would last. Not long, she told herself. He was just another rich man who could do as he pleased, and eventually, he'd tire of Rosie. And Kaitlyn would be there to make sure that the child was taken care of when he decided it was too much work.

And though she would be disappointed when he did, she would not be surprised.

Nick opted to sit in the back passenger compartment next to Rosie. Better than sitting next to Kaitlyn, who apparently thought so very little of him. Her lack of faith hurt more than he cared to admit.

So what if he'd never taken care of a child? How hard could it be? People did it all the time. And hopefully one of the staff members at the estate would know what to do. He was counting on it. But he certainly wasn't going to reveal that tidbit to Kaitlyn for her to use against him.

They'd made a quick stop at Kaitlyn's house for her to pack a bag of clothing. As they headed back through town, he said, "We should swing by the general store. We don't have any of the paraphernalia that babies require at the estate."

Kaitlyn met his gaze in the rearview mirror. "As much as I hate the idea of stopping, Rosie will need things. But at the first sign of trouble, we leave and make do with what you have at the house."

Acknowledging Kaitlyn's directive with a nod, he stroked Rosie's cheek with his finger. So soft, like a rose petal. Her little hands reached up and her tiny fingers wrapped around his index finger. A completely unfamiliar melting sensation in his midsection caught him by surprise and burned the backs of his eyes. Was this what it felt like when one became a parent?

But he wasn't a parent. Just a guardian, for now. Until Kaitlyn found somebody else better suited.

The bitter turn of his thoughts soured his stomach. It was hard to realize that the one person in Bristle Township he wanted to think highly of him didn't. He mentally shrugged and put up the mental wall of indifference that had served him well throughout his life.

For now, it was enough that Lexi had thought enough of him to entrust him with her child. And he didn't take that responsibility lightly, despite what Kaitlyn might believe.

Kaitlyn pulled into the parking lot of the fully stocked local general store that could rival any well-known branded superstore and parked next to the entrance.

"Stay put," she instructed before she got out and came around to the other side of the vehicle and opened the back passenger door.

Nick climbed out with Rosie safe in the car seat. Kaitlyn hustled them to the entrance. As they entered through the sliding glass doors, the bright lights assaulted him. He pushed the shopping cart with the baby carrier cradled between the handle and the back of the metal seat. The baby's eyes were wide, and her little mouth puckered around the pacifier.

He let out a low whistle. "There's everything you could want here."

Kaitlyn glanced at him before her gaze scanned the store. "You've never been in here, have you?"

"Collin does all the shopping." His father's valet ran the house along with his wife, the housekeeper.

Kaitlyn's mouth twisted with what could only be called derision.

He sighed. Another reason for her to think badly of him. But it wasn't his fault his family had money and he'd never had to shop for groceries.

"Come on," she said, hustling them forward. "Let's get this over with. I don't like being exposed. There are too many places our bad guy could hide."

Tension tightened his shoulder and neck muscles. They turned down an aisle filled with candy. He grabbed a bag of peppermint patties, his favorite, and tossed them in the basket. "Do you know where the baby stuff is?"

She paused, looked up at the signs hanging from the rafters, then pointed to her right. "This way."

He suppressed a grin, liking that she wasn't as familiar with the store as she'd wanted him to believe. Kaitlyn kept him and Rosie within arm's reach, which he appreciated, though he wished the reason wasn't because she worried the blond man would try to harm them. But, so far, they'd encountered very few people on this snowy night.

They found their way to the baby aisle. There was so much paraphernalia lining the shelves, he grew dizzy. There were so many choices. Blankets, bottles, formula, diapers, clothing and accessories galore. "How do we decide what we need?"

Kaitlyn grabbed a package of diapers and tossed them into the basket. "We definitely need these."

He looked at the package that read *stage four, twenty-two to thirty-seven pounds*. "I think those will be a wee bit too big."

She made a distinctly growling noise in her throat, grabbed the package and stuck it back on the shelf.

"They come in sizes by weight. Interesting," she said, as if speaking to herself and not him.

"Yes, they do." He stepped next to her, breathing in the heat of her skin as he tapped the stage two, twelve-to-sixteen-pounds package. "I'd say she weighs about twelve pounds."

Kaitlyn grabbed three packages. "We're going to need to feed her. I should call my mother."

"I know what to do." He took out the phone from the breast pocket of his overcoat and quickly did an online search for what was needed to care for a three-month-old baby. A list popped up. "Here we go. Formula."

They moved down the aisle.

"Do you think she has a sensitive stomach?"

Kaitlyn gave him a droll look. "How would I know?"

"Let's just believe she does. I'd rather be as gentle with her as possible," Nick said.

A little V appeared between Kaitlyn's eyebrows as she gave him a look he couldn't quite interpret. "Okay." She found a formula that met their criteria and read the instructions. "It says it just needs warm water in a bottle."

They walked over to the bottles. Once again, the choices were overwhelming. Plastic, glass, little plastic bags inside a plastic or glass container and then all the nipples. "Why is this so complicated?"

"I don't know," Kaitlyn said. "What does your phone say?"

"It just says bottles. Not which one, specifically."

"Then we'll get one of each and see which one she likes best."

"Now, that is a brilliant idea, Kaitlyn," he said. "Sounds like something I would've come up with."

Her hand stilled around a glass bottle. "They are only bottles, Nick. It's not like we're bonding."

Bonding. The word ricocheted through his mind. She'd made it clear she didn't like him. And he was tired of the challenge to make her like him. So bonding with Kaitlyn was not going to happen.

However, bonding with Rosie was another matter entirely. The little one had already tugged at his heart, and he didn't want to think about how much it would wreck him when he had to let her go. Until then, though, he was going to give her everything he had to give.

He filled the cart with toys, a monitor and bedding. He grabbed a tiny hat, tiny mittens and a warm-looking one-piece snowsuit for Rosie.

Nick stopped a salesclerk. "Do you have beds for babies?"

The woman's eyebrows rose. "You mean a crib?"

"Hi, Patty," Kaitlyn said. "I think that is what he means."

"Let me check the stockroom." Patty hurried away.

"She's only going to be with you for the night," Kaitlyn said.

He shrugged. "Whoever ends up with her will need this stuff." Though he couldn't imagine letting Rosie go.

A few moments later, Patty came back dragging a large box behind her. "Here you are."

"Thank you so much." Nick secured the box on the lower rack of the cart.

Shaking her head, Kaitlyn muttered, "We need a sign that says Wide Load."

He laughed. "Good one."

She pressed her lips together, but he could see the grin trying to escape, and it saddened him that she couldn't even let herself share a smile with him.

Resolved not to let her poor opinion of him derail his efforts to be the best guardian to baby Rosie he could be, he consulted the list on his phone. "It says we need onesies. What are onesies?"

"How would I know?" Kaitlyn muttered as she marched over to the baby clothing section. "Here you go." She pulled off a package that had the word *Onesies* written in big letters.

"Did you check the size?" Nick wasn't sure why he was poking at her. But he found it immensely satisfying when she made a face and put the package back, then rummaged through the selection until she found the correct size for a three-month-old.

"There." She tossed several in the basket along with another pink blanket. "Are we done yet?"

"Are you always an impatient shopper?" He was finding the experience fascinating.

"It's not my favorite activity," she said. "I'd rather be with my horse."

Of course she would. No surprise there. She rode in the county's mounted patrol and also grew up on a horse ranch. "You like horses more than you like people."

One corner of her mouth lifted. "Only more than some people."

Meaning him. Ignoring the sting of hurt, he pushed the cart toward the front of the store.

Kaitlyn led the way to the checkout counter. He was content to watch her walk with such purpose in her stride. Her gaze swung back and forth as if searching for a threat, while one hand rested on her utility belt and the other hovered over the butt of her sidearm. He had no doubt she'd face danger head-on, as she had in the hospital. She was a force to be reckoned with and a woman worth admiring. The man who captured her heart would be a blessed man, indeed.

He sighed and averted his gaze. But it wouldn't be him.

FOUR

Kaitlyn brought the department-issued vehicle to a halt at the foot of the steps to the Delaney's palatial home, which was lit up by large wall sconces that illuminated not only the entrance but the stone walls, as well. She turned off the engine and attempted to quell the nervous butterflies flopping around her tummy. Not an easy feat with Nick in the passenger seat next to her.

Why on earth was she nervous? This was an assignment. She'd been tasked with protecting Nick and Rosie. It wasn't like they were going to be alone for some sort of romantic evening.

The massive wooden front door opened, and an older man and woman hurried out. The estate's staff. Nick had called them on the drive up the mountain, alerting them to the situation.

Nick climbed out of the vehicle and went to the back, taking out the car seat holding the baby. Before he closed the rear passenger door, he said, "Pop open the back hatch, please."

Lips twisting at his instructions—like she didn't know to do that?—she shook her head. This was going to be a long night.

She hit the button that released the hatch to the back compartment where they'd stored their purchases from the general store and the bag she'd packed for herself. She hopped out and strode around to the back of the SUV.

"Deputy Kaitlyn Lanz, this is Collin McBride and his wife, Margaret." Nick gestured to the man and woman.

"Collin." Kaitlyn held out her hand. "We've met." She smiled at the older woman. "Margaret, nice to meet you."

"Likewise, Deputy." Margaret was a robust woman with silver hair pulled back into a bun. She wore slacks and a light-colored sweater beneath an apron. Her wary green-eyed gaze shifted to the baby carrier. "You really do have a baby with you. Nicolas, we thought perhaps you were joking."

Nick lifted the car seat higher. "No joke. This is Rosie. She and the deputy will be staying with us for the night."

"So you said," Margaret replied. Her brow wrinkled. "Where would you like them to be set up?"

"We'll put Rosie in the sitting room next to me and make up the bed in the yellow room at the top of the stairs for the deputy," Nick replied.

Margaret's eyebrows twitched as if the request was a surprise, but she nodded. "Of course. Let's get inside where it's warm."

"I'll take care of assembling the crib," Nick told Collin as the man hefted the large box in his hands.

"Very good, sir," Collin replied and headed inside.

Margaret took a bag of supplies in each arm and followed her husband.

"Shall we?" Nick asked as he grabbed one of the remaining bags in his free hand and carried the baby up the front staircase.

Retrieving the last bag and her duffel from the SUV, she locked the doors and hurried to follow him. She glanced up at the curved stone turrets at the corners of the grand structure that gave the home a fairy-tale castle, dreamlike facade. She hoped this didn't turn into a nightmare.

The foyer was as she remembered it. Cold marble floors, a wide staircase with a wrought-iron railing and walls adorned with paintings that would rival any museum. In the center of the entryway, a huge wooden table held a large vase filled with out-of-season flowers in a variety of spring colors.

Not one Christmas decoration could be seen. The place would be a sight to behold with some greenery and ornaments. Instead, it was very formal and not homey at all.

After handing off all but the bags containing their food, and the formula and bottles for Rosie, Nick led the way to the kitchen. While Rosie slept in her car seat, Nick laid out their feast. Sitting on a stool at the counter, Kaitlyn ate, aware that Nick had hardly looked at her since leaving the general store and he hadn't spoken unless necessary. Very odd.

Though, she had to admit, grabbing sandwiches had been a good idea. She'd been famished by the time they reached the Delaney estate. Nick seemed to be full of good ideas tonight. He was smart and more capable than she'd previously given him credit for.

In the past year or so, she'd limited the amount of time they spent together because she wasn't interested in his flirting. It made her uncomfortable, threw her off balance. And she didn't like being uncomfortable or off balance at all.

Even tonight, he'd started out like his usual self at the retirement/Christmas party. All flirty and pushing her buttons. But ever since he'd taken it upon himself to care for the baby, he'd behaved differently. The change was unsettling because it bent her expectations of him. When they'd arrived at the estate, he'd not once made any sort of flirtatious comment about joining him in his home. He'd been more concerned with the child.

Best to keep her guard up until she could be sure the change in him wasn't fleeting. She had no doubt that once the novelty of being a temporary guardian to little Rosie wore off, he'd revert to his carefree ways.

She pushed her empty chip bag aside and crumpled up the wrapper from her turkey sandwich. Nick picked up her trash and threw it away. She watched him as he moved around the kitchen, tidying up after their impromptu meal. Little Rosie, strapped in her car seat, sat on the counter, fast asleep. But there was a definite odor coming from her direction. That was not going to be fun.

"I think Rosie needs a clean diaper," she commented.

Nick nodded as he picked up the car seat and headed out of the kitchen. "Good thing there's a video online that shows how to change a diaper. I was hoping Margaret and Collin would be of help, but as Collin pointed out when I called earlier, they never had children."

Following him up the staircase, she asked, "They didn't help raise you and Ian?"

"No. We had a string of nannies over the years, but none stayed for long. The McBrides came into the Delaney employ when I was ten and Ian thirteen. A few years before my mother's death."

Her heart lurched. "You lost your mother young."

He paused on the landing at the top of the staircase.

He stared at her for a moment as she reached the top of the stairs also, then nodded. "Yes. She was fragile. She had Hodgkin's lymphoma. It wasn't caught in time to be cured."

Though Kaitlyn didn't know much about the disease, she could only imagine what the family had gone through. Her heart hurt for their loss. "I'm sorry. That must have been hard."

There was a flash of pain in his eyes before he turned toward the door to his right. "This will be your room."

She pushed open the door to reveal a large bedroom with a four-poster bed and an en suite bathroom. The walls were a pale yellow and the bedding had a cheery daisy motif. Her duffel bag sat waiting at the foot of the bed and looked out of place in the elegant room. There were high windows with lace curtains and a small desk suited to a female. "Very pretty. Whose room is this?"

Nick took a breath as if bracing himself. "This house is an exact replica of our estate in Massachusetts. My father had every room furnished and decorated exactly the way it was back East." He glanced into the room and then met her gaze. "This was my mother's favorite room. It hasn't been used since this place was built."

"That explains why Margaret was surprised when you said I'd be staying in here."

"Very observant of you," Nick said. "We keep all the rooms guest ready, even though we rarely have anyone stay here. The last time we had guests was when you, Chase and Ashley stayed last spring."

She remembered that night vividly. Her fellow deputies, Chase Fredrick and Ashley Willis, had ridden their horses from the woods to the estate, pursued by the minions of a crime lord who had been intent on silencing

Ashley because she'd witnessed a murder. Thanks to Nick's hospitality, they'd remained safe through the night and each had been given a bedroom on the main floor.

Rosie began to fuss. "Okay, sweetie," Nick cooed. "Let's go figure out how to change your diaper."

"I'll come with you," Kaitlyn said. For some reason, she was loath to be alone. Or, rather, to leave him alone with the baby. Yes, that was it. He would need her help. Not that she knew how to change a diaper, but still. She excelled at following directions.

Nick opened the door to a small room that had a dark wood desk and a wall of bookshelves filled with leather-bound volumes, as well as hardback fiction books. The boxed crib leaned against the desk, and the other purchases they'd made were neatly stacked on the window's bench seat.

A door stood open that led to another bedroom, obscured in shadows. Kaitlyn's eyebrows hiked up. "Is that your room?"

Setting the baby carrier on the floor, Nick nodded. "Yes. This way I'll be close by if Rosie needs anything."

Kaitlyn wasn't sure how she felt about going anywhere near Nick's inner sanctuary. But then she realized that if he tried anything funny, she could flatten him in an instant. Though she knew he wouldn't. In the whole year she'd known him, he'd never done anything inappropriate.

Just the flirting, which caused her no small amount of alarm. Mostly because of the way her blood would race and an answering attraction would ignite. She shook her head. She needed to get a grip. She was here because of the job and that was all.

Nick took off his sport jacket and hung it over a

comfortable-looking leather chair in the corner next to a reading table and lamp. For some reason, the cozy corner grabbed hold of Kaitlyn's insides and gave a sudden twist. She could picture Nick sitting there reading. What were his favorite books? Did they share any of the same tastes in literature?

She glanced at the hardback fiction collection and noted several authors she liked to read. Funny, she'd never considered they'd have anything in common.

He pushed up the sleeves of his dark green sweater, then picked up the changing pad he'd purchased and laid it out on the desk. He contemplated the baby. "She's sleeping so peacefully. I think we'll wait to change her diaper until she wakes up."

"Good call." It seemed right to let the baby sleep. But what did she know? While her friends had been baby-sitting to make money, she'd been giving riding lessons.

She looked around for something to do and her gaze landed on the crib. "Let's put the bed together."

"The box says no tools required," Nick said with a thumbs-up gesture.

Over the next hour, they muddled their way through assembling the crib. Kaitlyn had to admit it was actually fun working with Nick. He was all business. No flirting or impish grins to cause butterflies in her tummy. The weird thing was she kind of missed his playfulness. Silly, considering how annoying he could be.

Nick assembled and attached the cute zoo-animal mobile to the head of the crib. "Perfect."

Next he made sure the baby monitor and receiver worked.

Rosie stirred, squirming in her seat with little noises. Kaitlyn moved to the carrier and undid the straps holding Rosie in. For a second she hesitated to lift the little girl into her arms, but then she caught Nick watching her. If he could pick up the baby without mishap, then so could she.

Carefully, she untucked the blanket and scooped the baby into her hands, lifting her from the carrier, careful not to jostle her overmuch. Rosie was so lightweight, yet Kaitlyn hugged her close as if she were the heaviest and most precious object on Earth.

A shiver of something unfamiliar raced along her limbs, and her heart contracted in her chest with a tenderness that was unexpected and terrifying.

"Lay her on the changing pad," Nick instructed as he hovered at her elbow.

"I got it." Kaitlyn gently put Rosie on the pad. Keeping a hand on Rosie's tummy, she turned to Nick. "Now what?"

He grinned. "Time to watch that video on how to change a diaper."

Despite herself, Kaitlyn grinned back. "That would be wise."

Nick loaded the video on his phone and they successfully followed the instructions. They managed to change the baby's diaper, as well as put a clean onesie on her. Then Nick, using directions off the internet, swaddled the baby in a new blanket and put her on her back in the crib. Kaitlyn had never seen this side of him before and found him quite endearing. But she didn't want to be endeared. Letting anyone close was a risk she wasn't willing to take.

"Maybe we should put the other blanket on her, too. Rosie might like to have Lexi's scent wrapped around her," Kaitlyn suggested. "It helped to comfort my dog,

Magpie, when she was a puppy." The golden retriever puppy had been a Christmas present. Mom had taken one of Kaitlyn's old barn jackets and let the puppy sleep on it as a way to comfort Magpie when Kaitlyn wasn't there.

"Good idea," Nick said. "The blanket might make Rosie not feel so lonely and afraid. I've read that the sense of smell is closely linked to memory."

His tender gaze was disconcerting. She turned away and plucked the blanket from the carrier. The edge of an envelope stuck out from beneath the seat's cushion. Dropping the blanket back into the seat, she lifted the envelope from the carrier.

"What's that?" he asked.

"Not sure." She held it by the corner. "It was stuck behind the cushion."

"Open it," Nick said.

Carefully slipping her fingernail beneath the flap, she opened the envelope and pulled out two pieces of paper. The first one was a handwritten note to Nick. She glanced up at him. "It's to you."

"Read it."

She read it aloud. "'Dear Nick, if you're reading this, then I'm in trouble. Maybe even dead. I'm sorry to drop this news on you out of the blue. But you're the only one I can trust. I know you'll do what's right. Please take care of her. I love her with all my heart. You are a good man. Lexi.'"

They already knew Lexi had been headed to Nick for help. But why? And who had she been running from?

"What is the other paper?" Nick asked, his voice strained as if he were holding back some emotion.

Kaitlyn opened the trifolded paper and her breath caught. A birth certificate. She quickly scanned the document. Lexi Eng was named as the mother of baby Rosie Eng. But it was the name of the father that wrenched Kaitlyn's heart.

The name typed in the space for the father was *Nicholas Delaney.*

Her hands shook and her stomach dropped. Nick was the baby's father. It had his signature and everything. She turned the document around for Nick to see. Anger made her hands shake. "Care to explain why you lied to me?"

"What? Lie?" Nick grabbed the paper and looked at it. There was puzzlement in his eyes as they lifted to meet hers. "This is fake. There's no way this is an official document. Those require ID. I'm not Rosie's father."

"But you signed it," Kaitlyn pointed out.

He shook his head. "No, I didn't. That's not my signature and they spelled my name wrong. There's no *h* in my name." He stalked to his sport coat and took his wallet out from the inside pocket, then extracted his driver's license. "Here. See for yourself."

She inspected his license and discovered he was telling the truth.

The relief coursing through her veins was disturbing. There was no reason she should have a reaction one way or another about his personal life. If he were truly the child's father, it shouldn't matter to her. However, unaccountably, it did. She was glad to learn he wasn't. And what did that say about her?

But who was Rosie's father?

"I'm not in the habit of lying." Nick turned away from Kaitlyn. He hated seeing the suspicion and wariness in her gaze. How could she think he'd lie to her? And why would he? If he'd fathered this baby, he'd own up to the fact. Yes, there had been times when he'd behaved recklessly and irresponsibly as a young man, but maturity had taught him the importance of responsibility and caution.

It hurt that she thought so little of him.

Returning his wallet to his coat pocket gave him a moment to take a breath and calm the inner turmoil. Her approval or disapproval shouldn't affect him so deeply.

"Why would Lexi name you as the father and go to such lengths as to make a fake birth certificate to perpetuate the lie?"

Facing Kaitlyn, Nick arched an eyebrow. "Because, unlike you, she believed in me. She knows I have the means and that I would help her. For whatever reason, she didn't want to name the biological father."

A V appeared between Kaitlyn's blue eyes. "Or she was hoping to bilk you out of some money."

"No. I refuse to believe she would do that. She had a successful career as a graphic designer. Her fear and those men who tried to kill her were real."

He moved to pick up the blanket that Kaitlyn had left in the carrier and placed it gently over Rosie. The baby's little brow furrowed for a moment and he held his breath, thinking he'd woken her, but then her breathing evened out and her little face relaxed.

A welling of tenderness and affection flooded his system. He reaffirmed to himself he'd do whatever necessary to protect this baby.

With the baby monitor's receiver in hand, he motioned for Kaitlyn to join him in the hall and closed the door to the sitting room. "It's late. We should get some rest."

Kaitlyn's lips twisted. "You do understand that I have a duty to find the baby's father."

"Why? Obviously, Lexi didn't want to name the father. There had to be a reason," Nick stated.

"I appreciate you wanting to do right by this woman and her child," Kaitlyn said.

"Do you?" At every turn it seemed more that she wanted to put a wedge between him and the baby.

"Yes. But we don't have all the facts here and I will find them," she said. "If Rosie's father is not fit to care for Rosie, then she'll become a ward of the state and enter foster care. Finding her biological father is the right thing to do."

"And you have always done the right thing," he said, even as he knew her words were true.

The baby's father had a right to know about Rosie. But if the man was abusive or a deadbeat, then Nick would make sure the man had no access to the innocent child left in Nick's care. Nor would he allow Rosie to end up in the system, not when he could provide for her. He sent up a quick prayer that Lexi would recover soon and they could sort out this mess and discover why someone had wanted her dead.

An earsplitting siren ripped through the house. Instinctively, Nick met Kaitlyn's startled gaze.

"Someone is trying to break in," he shouted.

She pointed to the room they'd just exited. "Stay with the baby," she yelled. She pivoted and raced down the hall with her gun in hand, then disappeared down the staircase.

FIVE

Heart pounding with adrenaline, Nick lifted a prayer of protection for Kaitlyn as she headed downstairs to confront whatever threat had set off the security alarms. When she was out of sight, Nick rushed back to the room that was now serving as Rosie's nursery. The soft glow of the night-light kept the darkness at bay. He lifted the crying baby from the crib. Her screams nearly matched the alarm in pitch. He held her to his chest, wishing there was some way to protect her young ears from the noise, but the assault to their senses was grating.

Carrying Rosie, he hurried to a secret panel in the hallway wall that led to a panic room. He'd never used the space before and was surprised by how well stocked his father kept it. A cot with blankets, bottles of water and nonperishable dry goods were stacked in one corner. But even with the door closed, the muffled shrieking of the alarm was no less unnerving.

He took some grim satisfaction from knowing whoever had triggered the alarm, either by attempting to scale the wall or the wrought-iron gate, had suffered a shock. Both the wall and gate were armed with electricity.

Within moments, the ear-piercing sound of the alarm ceased. Though Rosie continued to wail.

"Shhhh, little one," Nick cooed as he gently bounced her. "You're safe. I've got you."

Rosie squirmed against him, burrowing her face into him, creating a warm spot over his heart.

Then he heard the faint sound of the sirens of the Bristle Township Sheriff's Department. Nick was grateful to know that backup was arriving for Kaitlyn. He worried that she would be out there trying to deal with the bad guys by herself. The men who'd attacked Lexi had proved they were willing to do violence. That they hadn't succeeded in killing Lexi didn't mean that they would hesitate to kill Kaitlyn. His stomach knotted. Dread gripped him at the thought of something happening to her.

He tightened his hold on the baby. Her cries softened to hiccups. He could feel the wetness of Rosie's tears soaking through his sweater and T-shirt beneath. The emotions cascading through him were unfamiliar and humbling. His chest expanded as if stretching to accommodate all the love filling his heart. He'd never thought he was capable of such feelings.

A noise outside the room sent a spike of wariness zipping through him.

"Nick!"

The sound of Kaitlyn's voice relieved him, but the anxiousness tingeing it tempered his relief. She was alive, but was she wounded? He quickly opened the secret panel.

Kaitlyn started. "What in the world? A panic room?" She gave her head a shake. "Figures. Are you two okay?"

"We're good." His gaze quickly traveled over Kaitlyn for any sign of injury. "You?"

"I'm fine." Behind her he saw Collin and his wife hovering in the doorway.

"It was two men," Collin said. "We have them on video. But their faces were hidden with ski masks. They were spooked when the alarm went off and probably a little scorched by the electric fence."

"Thank you," Nick said. "I believe I heard police sirens?"

"Yes. I called the sheriff. Plus, the alarm system alerted the department," Kaitlyn stated.

"Collin, would you please let the sheriff in when he arrives?"

"Yes." Collin and his wife moved away from the door.

"We have to figure out what these men are after," Kaitlyn said.

"Isn't it obvious?" Nick said. He moved to the changing table and went about the task of changing the baby's diaper. "They want Rosie." And they weren't going to get her. Not as long as he had breath in his body.

Kaitlyn's skeptical expression suggested she didn't agree with him. "I have to dig into Lexi's life. Find out what she was involved in that would cause her and Rosie to be targeted. You need to tell me everything you know about her."

"We were friends a long time ago." As he swaddled Rosie in her pink rose-covered blanket, he thought back to those days in New York three years ago. "I met her at a charity fundraising event put on by a popular magazine. She had done some work for the publication. We started talking. I know she was born in Singapore. That her father passed when she was young. We had the death of a parent in common."

He picked up Rosie and gently rocked her. She stared

up at him with dark, trusting eyes. "I don't recall where Lexi's mother resides. When I knew Lexi, she shared a two-bedroom apartment with two of her college roommates, whom I never met. I secured her an interview with a friend who owned an advertising firm. She was a graphic artist, so it seemed like a good match. Last I heard, she was offered the job and moved to DC."

Kaitlyn stepped closer to softly touch Rosie's dark smattering of hair. "You have no idea who Lexi might be involved with now?"

"No, I don't. We didn't keep in touch," he said. "Do you think the baby's father is the one behind all this?"

Kaitlyn frowned. "If those men had wanted the baby, why did they leave her in the back seat of Lexi's car? If their intent was to kidnap Rosie, wouldn't they have taken her and not tried to take Lexi?"

"But the man in the hospital did try to take Rosie," Nick reminded her and shuddered at the memory. His head hurt with all the unanswered questions. Only Lexi could give them the answers they sought. "We should check with the hospital and see how Lexi's doing."

"I'm sure the sheriff will update us." Kaitlyn walked over to where Rosie's diaper bag sat on the desk. She lifted it up and looked inside. "This and the car seat are the only items we took from the crash site. But we didn't find anything of value in the diaper bag."

"The men also searched the bag after they caused Lexi to crash her car," he reminded her. "The contents were strewn all over the ground."

"True." She set the bag down. "Do you think they want the birth certificate?" She picked up the car seat and dismantled the lining, inspecting every inch of the carrier.

"Why would they? Other than the fact the certificate is fake, I don't see what significance it could have to anyone else."

"Maybe they just want to get their hands on Rosie so they have leverage against Lexi." Kaitlyn lost interest in the car seat and moved toward the door. "I should talk to Alex."

After Kaitlyn walked out of the room, Nick gently laid Rosie in her crib. She'd fallen back to sleep. He ran the outside edge of his finger over the petal-soft skin of her cheek. "Don't worry, little one. I won't let anything happen to you."

A quick search of the internet gave him the phone number for the Boston protection agency his father trusted. If Nick had known of one closer, he'd have called them, so the next best thing was to call Trent Associates. Because it was late on the East Coast, he left a detailed message with his needs. For now, he would have to be satisfied with the sheriff's department and the house's security system. He trusted Kaitlyn would do her best to keep them safe.

Needing something to do, Nick tidied the room. As he picked up the diaper bag, he contemplated what Kaitlyn had said. Other than Rosie, the car seat and diaper bag were the only possessions of Lexi's they'd brought home. He ran his hand over the inside of the bag, feeling the lining for any hidden objects. Nothing. The bag had many compartments and he checked each one. Deep in one of the outside zippered pockets, his fingers snagged on a thin chain wedged into the seam.

With a little effort, he managed to hook the chain over his finger and extract a small butterfly-shaped pendant on a delicate gold chain from the pocket. It was clearly a costume trinket. Something one would see for sale on the sidewalk along Central Park in the summer. Certainly not worth all this trouble.

Maybe it was something Lexi had seen and bought to eventually give her daughter. He stepped to the crib and hung the necklace on the mobile so that Rosie would be able to see it hanging over her, a reminder that her mother loved her.

Taking the baby monitor receiver, he went downstairs to find Kaitlyn talking to Sheriff Alex Trevino and Deputy Daniel Rawlings in the entryway. Both men were in uniforms covered by heavy coats. A dusting of snow clung to Alex's shoulders and hair, while the brim of Daniel's beige Stetson dripped with melting snow. Apparently, the winter storm raged on outside.

Nick shook hands with the two men. "Alex, I have to thank you for sending Kaitlyn home with me and Rosie. She kept us safe. She reacted swiftly to the security alarms."

Kaitlyn stared at him. "I was doing my job."

"And you did it very well," he said.

"Uh, thank you." She turned her attention to Alex. "Any news on Lexi's condition?"

"I talked to the doctor an hour ago. He said she's still critical. The next forty-eight hours are crucial."

A heaviness weighed on Nick's heart. He silently prayed for Lexi's healing.

"In light of this attempt to breach the premises," Alex said, "I can have Daniel stay with you."

"Having two deputies might be a bit of overkill, don't you think? Besides, that would put the department down by two people," Nick said. "Unless, of course, Kaitlyn would like to leave?"

She shook her head. "Now that the intruders know

that there's no way to get beyond the perimeter, I think we can consider the house safe," Kaitlyn said. "But I will stay with Rosie and Nick, just in case these criminals come back."

Nick let out a silent sigh of relief. Not that he didn't think Daniel would be competent enough to protect them. It was more that Nick preferred to have Kaitlyn. And he didn't want to look too closely at why that was.

"That's a good plan. We can't be too careful," Alex said. He turned to the deputy beside him. "Daniel, you can go relieve Chase at the hospital."

"Yes, sir." Daniel left through the front door.

"How's the baby?" Alex asked.

"She's sleeping," Nick responded. "The alarms were jarring, but she's resilient."

Alex smiled. "Good to hear. I think for now it's best that Rosie stay here for the duration until we arrest these men and find out what is going on."

"Of course I will keep her," Nick was quick to assure him. There was no way anyone was going to tear this child from him now. Though he knew it was going to hurt when he eventually had to give her back to Lexi. He wanted to unite Rosie with her mother, and he would make sure that they were both set for life.

Kaitlyn showed Alex the letter and the fake birth certificate. "We're not sure what this all means."

"That's not my signature," Nick informed him and held his breath as he waited for Alex's thoughts. Would he believe him? Or would the sheriff be suspicious of him, like Kaitlyn was?

"Someone went to a lot of trouble to make it appear as if you're Rosie's father." Alex put both pieces of paper in an evidence bag. "I'll see if Hannah can pull any prints off the certificate to see if anyone other than Lexi and you two handled it."

Nick was thankful for his friend's belief in him. If only Kaitlyn had as much faith.

After Alex left and the alarm system was reactivated, Nick and Kaitlyn went upstairs. They paused outside the room she would be sleeping in.

"Good night, Kaitlyn. Try to get some rest," Nick said.

She hesitated. "I'd like to check in on Rosie."

Surprised, Nick smiled to himself. For all of Kaitlyn's assertions that she didn't know anything about children, she'd become attached to the little girl, too. And knowing that gladdened Nick's heart. "Of course."

They walked to the end of the hall and quietly slipped into the nursery. In the low light of the plug-in night-light, they both stood beside the crib watching the tiny swaddled girl sleep.

"You're really good with her," Kaitlyn said in a low voice.

"You're marveling at my swaddling powers," he quipped softly.

Her small laugh was gratifying.

"Yes, that's it." She stepped back. "Good night, Nick."

Nick watched her stride from the room, shoulders back and head high. It must have cost her to give him a compliment. And the warmth of knowing she'd had a good thought toward him made him sad. Because no matter what happened, he couldn't let himself fall for Deputy Kaitlyn Lanz. Not if he hoped to keep his heart safe from the inevitable pain of not being enough.

As Kaitlyn lay in bed, every noise sent her heart hammering. A few times she heard Rosie, but she would quiet down quickly. Several times Kaitlyn arose, padded downstairs in her sweats and sweatshirt to check the ground-floor windows and doors. Though she logically knew that there was no way anyone could get onto the property without triggering the alarm again, she couldn't find rest.

Near two in the morning, Kaitlyn heard the barest hint of noise outside her door. Quickly, she put on her shoes and cracked open her door to see Nick heading downstairs carrying the baby monitor receiver. She followed him.

She found Nick, dressed in loose-fitting pants and a long-sleeve T-shirt that hugged his chest muscles, in the dojo on the lowest level of the house. To keep from staring at the handsome man, she studied the room. She'd been here once before, when Nick had taken her on a tour of the house. The large room with mats on the floor held all sorts of martial arts training equipment, from nunchucks to combat sticks.

Without a word, Nick tossed her a set of padded gloves. For the next hour, they sparred, trading punches and jabs that stopped short of hurting. She was sure he was pulling his blows, just as she was, to avoid injury. Neither spoke, as if somehow conversation would ruin the experience.

She had to admit, letting off steam from the horrible day was cathartic. They both needed this. When they were both breathing heavily and sweating, they stopped. Nick bowed and then peeled off his gloves. She followed suit. They headed upstairs once again with no words necessary. She'd found the experience both exhilarating and disconcerting. Not to mention she was impressed with his skills.

The next morning, after dressing in jeans and a fresh

sweater, Kaitlyn went in search of Nick. She found him standing beside Rosie's crib. The baby made little cooing sounds as she sucked on her pacifier and watched the mobile hanging over her head. Sunlight flooded the small sitting room serving as the nursery. It was a bluebird day, the air cleaned by the previous night's snowfall, leaving the sky an intense, cloudless blue.

"Did you get any sleep?" she asked as she stopped next to him. After the horrific day and their sparring match late last night, she'd found rest for a few hours.

He looked even more handsome today than last night in jeans and a sweater in a russet color. His dark hair looked freshly washed and combed back. The scent of aftershave on his clean-shaven jaw teased her nose, musky and masculine. Her heart rate ticked up a notch. She should step away but found her feet wouldn't budge.

He smiled at her. "Some. You?"

She couldn't help but return the smile. "Same."

"The nurse at the hospital said we should take Rosie in to see the pediatrician," Nick said.

"That is true." Kaitlyn thought about it for a moment, then said, "Better to ask Dr. Olson to make a house visit. I'll make the call and see when he can come out."

Using her smartphone, she looked up the local pediatrician's office number and dialed. She explained the situation and what was needed to the receptionist. The receptionist placed her on hold and returned a few moments later to say that Dr. Olson would be out to the estate within the hour.

"Last night I called Trent Associates, a security firm out of Boston that my father has used often. They will send operatives as soon as possible," Nick told her as they waited for the doctor to arrive.

Had he decided she wasn't capable of protecting them? "That's good."

She could return to her job. She hadn't wanted to take this assignment anyway. Then why did his hiring someone else sting?

Nick broke the silence. "What would you normally be doing on a Saturday morning?"

"When not on duty, I'd be doing chores at my family's ranch," she replied. She'd checked in with her parents last night, letting them know where she would be staying for the foreseeable future. But apparently she hadn't needed to pack quite as much clothing.

"Chores?" Nick's nose wrinkled. "Like what?"

"Mucking out the stalls, exercising the horses," she replied. "We board and train horses." Though she suspected he already was aware.

"I'd like to see your family's ranch sometime," he said.

She glanced at him to gauge if he was just being his flirty self or if the statement arose from something else. He wasn't looking at her, but rather out the window, as if trying to picture her ranch. Why would he want to see her family home? A flutter of something odd, something akin to delight, made her heart rate tick up. She wasn't sure what to make of his statement or her reaction.

"What about you?" she asked to distract him from asking any more questions about her. The thought of telling him details about herself made her twitchy and uncomfortable. "What would you normally be doing if you hadn't had a baby dropped into your arms?" Most likely off on some grand adventure.

He met her gaze with a smile. "Skiing. Days like this

are perfect for taking a few runs down the backside of Eagle Peak Mountain."

"Ah." That sounded right. Those runs were black diamond, the hardest on the mountain. Of course, he'd be daring enough to take them on.

His eyebrows rose. "Do you ski?"

She shook her head. "Not really. I've had some lessons, but I prefer horseback riding to having thin rails strapped to my feet."

Nick chuckled. "Well, we will have to hit the slopes together. The only way to really learn to ski is by doing."

She had a feeling that was how Nick lived his life. Doing whatever struck his interest. Like the baby. But how long would little Rosie be able to keep Nick engaged?

"And the only way you'll learn to ride a horse is by doing," she shot back, remembering his lack of enthusiasm for horses when she and Chase had brought Ashley to the estate on horseback.

"You're not wrong," he said. "Would you teach me to ride?"

The twinkle in his dark eyes set alarms bells clanging in her head. What sort of ploy was this? "Are you being serious?"

"I am," he said. "I would like to know how to sit a horse and to be able to go on rides on the many trails around here."

"I'm sure something can be arranged." Her father could teach him. Or Alex or someone other than her.

Collin appeared in the doorway. "Dr. Olson is at the gate. Should I let him in?"

"Please do," Nick said. "You can escort him here, if you wouldn't mind."

"Not at all."

Nick checked Rosie's diaper. "She's still dry."

"When does she get fed?" Kaitlyn asked.

"I gave her a bottle first thing this morning," he replied. "I downloaded a book on how to take care of babies onto my laptop. Very interesting reading, with clear directions on feeding schedules, sleeping schedules and all sorts of interesting things."

Uh. He was really getting into this, even more than she'd thought. "Do you always dive headlong into everything you do?"

He cocked his head. "I suppose so, when I find something that interests me."

"Must be nice to have the luxury to do that," she said.

He shrugged. "I can't help the circumstance to which I was born."

"No, I suppose not." Did he realize how blessed he was to have the opportunities that having come from such a well-off family afforded him?

"Hello." Dr. Olson stepped into the room. He was tall and had thinning dark hair with flecks of gray and a defined widow's peak at the top of his forehead. His blue-gray eyes were kind as they swept over them. In his hand he carried a black bag, which he set on the desk.

"Thank you for coming." Nick shook the doctor's hand. "This is Rosie."

"Isn't she a beauty?" Dr. Olson opened his bag and took out his stethoscope. "I'll give her a good once-over to make sure all is as it should be."

Nick and Kaitlyn moved out of the way to let the doctor examine Rosie.

"This baby is healthy," Dr. Olson announced. "And

you've done a good job setting her up in a safe environment so quickly."

"We appreciate you coming out here," Kaitlyn said. "I'm sure you're very busy."

"Never too busy to take care of a baby." He ran the back of a finger down Rosie's fat cheek and made her coo. "And you two are doing a wonderful job."

Kaitlyn didn't feel like she'd done anything to help the child. It had all been Nick. He'd taken to tending to Rosie like an expert. She struggled to believe Rosie was the first baby he'd ever held or taken care of. Watching him with the baby stirred up unfamiliar emotions inside, and she didn't know what to do with them other than shove them away.

"I will leave you my card," Dr. Olson said. "If you have any issues or questions, don't hesitate to call, and I will come back out. Keep up the good work." He handed Rosie to Kaitlyn.

Flustered, Kaitlyn felt her heart race, and her muscles tensed. She worked hard to hide the fact that she felt inadequate caring for the baby. But holding the infant close created unexpected havoc with her heart.

Nick walked the doctor out, leaving Kaitlyn and Rosie alone.

Swaying, Kaitlyn hummed a Christmas carol. Tenderness flooded her veins. For some inexplicable reason, tears burned the backs of her eyes.

Nick returned, his gaze disconcerting as he watched her and Rosie. She never would have imagined Nick would be so willing to take in the child, let alone be attentive to Rosie.

That he was also attentive to Kaitlyn left her feeling off balance in his presence.

"Why haven't you decorated the house for Christmas?" Kaitlyn asked to shift his focus away from herself.

"I honestly hadn't thought much about it." He straightened the blankets in Rosie's crib. "With Ian and Dad out of the country, decorating seemed pointless." He grinned. "But now that there's a child in the house, we should decorate. Are you game?"

His grin hit Kaitlyn square in the solar plexus, prompting a quick "I'd like that."

He waggled his eyebrows. "This will be fun."

Fun? Her mouth dried. What had she just agreed to?

"But first… I smell breakfast," Nick said and led the way downstairs.

A loud buzzing noise from outside the house raised the hairs at the back of her neck. "What is that?"

Nick's perplexed expression mirrored her own bafflement. "I don't know. A swarm of bees?"

Handing Rosie off to him, she said, "Not likely in winter."

Thankful she'd tucked her sidearm into her hip holster when she'd left her room this morning, she put her hand on the grip. Slowly she opened the front door to a blast of cold air.

She stepped out the door, searching for the source of the sound. The noise faded, indicating whatever was making it had moved to the back of the house.

"Wait," Nick said as she started down the front stairs. "The back door would be quicker."

Reversing, she hurried after him through the kitchen to the door that faced the rear of the mansion. Margaret and Collin stared, clearly alarmed.

"You all need to stay back," Kaitlyn instructed as she cautiously opened the door and peered out. A path had been shoveled through the snow, which was at least a foot deep and covered most of the patio and the furniture, to the greenhouse a few yards away.

The buzzing sounded overhead. She stepped out onto the patio and looked up, shielding the bright sunlight from her eyes with her free hand.

There! A quadcopter, named for the four rotors on the four corners of the civilian drone, hovered over the house.

Her lungs filled with crisp, cold air that did nothing to stem the tide of anger washing through her. Apparently, the men who were after Lexi and had tried to break in last night were surveilling the house with the camera attached to the drone, no doubt planning their next attack.

She raised her weapon and aimed at the quadcopter. The thing quickly veered away and flew out of range, disappearing over the tops of the trees, confirming her suspicion that the drone had been outfitted with a camera. Apparently one with real-time viewing, not just recording.

From the direction the drone was going, Kaitlyn decided the bad guys must have hiked around the perimeter looking for a way in.

"Should we be worried?" Nick asked when she re-entered the kitchen.

By the tone of his voice, she could tell the question was rhetorical. She wanted to reassure him, but she couldn't, not with her own concern crowding her chest. "Unfortunately, I don't think these men are going to stop anytime soon."

But what was it exactly they were after?

SIX

After informing Alex about the drone, tension stretched Kaitlyn's nerves taut. What did these men want? Rosie? But why? What was it about the baby that would lead these men to be so determined to get to her?

"Would you like to eat at the counter or in the dining room?" Margaret's voice shook slightly.

Kaitlyn sympathized with the other woman. Margaret and Collin were in danger along with Nick and Rosie by virtue of the fact they resided on the estate.

"Counter's fine," Nick said as he balanced Rosie in his arms and took a seat at the counter. His mood had been subdued by the very real threat hovering over them.

Kaitlyn took a seat and tried for normalcy. "Do I smell bacon?"

"You do. And fresh veggie omelets." Margaret placed plates filled with two slices of bacon and an omelet in front of Kaitlyn and Nick. "Eat before it gets cold."

"Yes, ma'am," Nick said. He glanced at Kaitlyn. "Would you like me to say grace?"

"Please," Kaitlyn replied.

"Lord, we thank You for this food and ask for Your blessing and Your protection. In Jesus's name, amen."

"Amen," Kaitlyn murmured. Though she wasn't hungry, she didn't want to be rude by not eating the food set before her. With every bite, however, her appetite grew. She needed her strength, she rationalized as she ate the whole plateful. "The omelet is so good. The veggies are super fresh. Where did you get them?"

"Out back," Margaret said. "Nick has a greenhouse full of veggies and flowers."

Kaitlyn nearly choked on her food. She swallowed quickly. "What?" She turned to stare at Nick. She'd seen the glass structure but hadn't thought much about it. "You have a greenhouse?"

"I like growing things," he stated. "And it's wonderful to have fresh produce year-round."

Kaitlyn didn't know what to say. Never would she have thought he'd be a gardener. "Interesting choice of hobby."

Nick smiled but looked away. "Plants don't judge."

"I'm not judging you," she said quickly. "If you find joy in gardening, that's wonderful."

"Gives me depth," he shot back.

She hated to admit it, but yes. Before now she'd considered him very superficial and lacking in complexity. But apparently there was more to Nick than she'd known. The past twenty-four hours had cracked open the box she'd relegated him to. And she wasn't quite sure what to make of it or the seeds of respect germinating inside her.

"Don't let him fool you," Margaret said. "Nick here is a Certified Master Gardener."

"Really?" No way would Kaitlyn have guessed.

Nick shrugged. "I took a course through the Colorado Certified Nursery Professionals program. It's not a big deal."

She'd always wondered what he did with his time. "I think this is a big deal." She held his dark gaze and for a moment couldn't breathe. There was something there in his eyes that made her heart pound and her blood race. "I'd like to see your garden sometime."

He wiped his mouth with a napkin before saying, "Then let me show you."

Shaking her head, she said, "Not a good idea."

Nick tucked in his chin. "Didn't last night prove the bad guys can't get onto the estate?"

True. But an anxious flutter in her chest demanded caution. Who knew what the bad guys could put on the next drone that flew over? "I'd prefer we stayed inside."

Resignation shone in the dark depths of his eyes. "Of course. You're the boss."

Was he mocking her? Nick's smile appeared genuine. Still, his words made her defenses rise, but she held herself in check. The situation was stressful enough without her unnecessarily adding to it. He'd accepted her mandate and that was that.

"How about we bring the Christmas decorations down from the attic?" he asked.

Clearly, he needed something to focus on other than the danger lurking outside the fenced estate. She couldn't deny him the concession. "Sure."

His pleased smile made her chest ache with a strange sort of happiness. When had she allowed him to have so much power over her? And what was she going to do about it?

A lump formed in Nick's throat. He and Kaitlyn stood in the dining room surrounded by the plethora of boxes marked *Christmas*. Sunlight streamed through the floor-to-ceiling windows, shining on the ornaments inside the boxes.

It had taken nearly two hours to bring all the boxes down from the attic. Rosie slept upstairs, and the baby monitor receiver sat nearby.

The reminder of his past had Nick choking up.

When he was young, decorating the house had been something his mother did, and she had shooed away her sons on the pretext they would be in the way of her creativity. But Nick had enjoyed watching his mother transform the house into something whimsical.

After her death, the house staff took over preparing the house for the holidays. With his father and Ian out of the country, Nick had told Collin not to bother. But now Nick wanted to make the house feel homey. For Rosie. And, to be honest, for Kaitlyn. But he was out of his element here.

"Where should we start?" he asked Kaitlyn. "I have to admit this is my first time being the one in charge of decorating the house."

Kaitlyn arched an eyebrow. "No kidding? Who would've thunk?"

He made a face at her. "Mock all you like. I'm doing it now."

Curiosity brightened her eyes. He wasn't about to reveal the painful truth that his mother hadn't really wanted to be bothered with her children, so he held her gaze with a steady look, hoping she'd let it go.

Finally, she looked around as if contemplating the best strategic way to go about decorating. He could practically see the wheels in her agile and quick mind spinning.

"Well, first off…" She met his gaze, her pretty eyes

sincere. "You don't have a Christmas tree, so there is that issue."

"An issue easily remedied." He took his phone from his pocket. "I'll call a local Christmas tree farm and have them deliver one."

"*I'll* call the Howards' Tree Farm." Kaitlyn dug her phone out of the pocket of her jeans, allowing her pink sweater to hike up slightly to reveal her holster and sidearm. "They own a Christmas tree farm outside of town. I trust them. Riley and his son, Trevor, ride on the mounted patrol."

Nick suppressed a smile. She liked being in control. "That's fine."

A few moments later, she hung up. "Trevor will bring us a tree."

"I'll let Collin know." Nick liked that she used the term *us*, though he didn't have any illusions that Kaitlyn gave some sort of significance to the word. There was no *us*. They were not together, like a couple. And the quicker he got that through his thick skull, the better. Kaitlyn barely tolerated him. There was no way he'd ever win her heart.

Why he even contemplated doing something so reckless was a mystery.

If he wanted to take the risk and give his heart, it should be to someone who accepted him, flaws and all.

And that was not Kaitlyn.

Kaitlyn watched Nick contemplate a stunning glass orb with swirls of glittery colors inside. There was a sadness to his expression that tugged at her and made her want to see his smile again. Her attraction to the man both annoyed and confused her. "Should we check on Rosie?"

His expression shifted, the sadness retreating to be replaced with an amused sort of joy. He grinned and waggled his eyebrows. "She's growing on you."

Kaitlyn's pulse unaccountably began to race. She struggled to calm it down. She didn't like that his grin made her heart beat faster. "Rosie is cute."

Her gaze strayed out the tall windows. And so was he, but she wouldn't ever admit that out loud.

She'd worked long and hard to keep herself free of romantic entanglements, because after what had happened ten years ago, she wasn't about to risk her heart ever again. And certainly not with this man she didn't fully trust to honor his commitments.

A section of the tree line surrounding the back of the house went up in a swoosh of flames. For a moment, Kaitlyn couldn't believe what she was seeing. Her heart stalled, then pounded in large, booming beats. "Fire!"

"We have to put it out!" Nick hurried to the window.

"This could be a ruse to flush us out," she said. "You need to secure Margaret, Collin and Rosie in the safe room."

Without a word, Nick raced to do as she'd commanded.

Dialing the sheriff's department as she ran for the back door, Kaitlyn reached the emergency dispatcher. "Fire at Delaney estate. South side tree line. Tell the sheriff suspects may be on scene outside of the fence surrounding the estate. Be cautious."

She cracked open the door. There was no way anyone could be on the electrified fence surrounding the estate, but she couldn't be sure there wasn't a sniper positioned out there on a nearby hillside waiting to pick her off. But to what end?

Even with her or Nick dead, the bad guys wouldn't be able to gain access to the mansion or to Rosie.

Cautiously, she edged out the door. When no bullet slammed into her, she let out a relieved breath. She could only guess that the bad guys planned to infiltrate the grounds when the gate opened for the fire department. She'd make sure that didn't happen.

Collin joined her. "There are fire extinguishers in the greenhouse and two extra-long hoses. We keep the water temperature tepid for the plants."

Grateful for the assist, she led the way to the glass-enclosed structure. Inside the greenhouse, warmth encased her. She barely spared a glance at the beautiful blooms used to decorate the inside of the mansion and the long rows of vegetables growing in planters. Collin reached a cabinet and flung the doors open. Inside were multiple types, shapes and sizes of extinguishers. Two coiled, heavy-duty hoses hung on hooks.

"Take two extinguishers and protect the house from cinders," Kaitlyn instructed Collin.

"Let's grab the hoses," Nick said as he stormed into the greenhouse. "We can do this."

Kaitlyn nodded, appreciating his can-do attitude but concerned for his safety. "You should be inside."

"Don't start with me, Kait," he said as he reached for a hose. "We're doing this together."

Marveling at his audacity and bravery, she tucked away the approval and hoisted a hose over her shoulder.

"This way." Nick, with the other hose over his own shoulder, led her back outside and through the snow to find the water faucet that had been encased in a foam-

and-plastic cover to keep it from freezing. He yanked the cover off. "We'll have to hook the hoses together to reach the tree line."

She nodded. They worked well together as they connected the ends of the two hoses.

She fumbled with the hose and pulled, straining to make the slog with the connected hoses across the snow-covered lawn toward the trees at the back of the property. Heat rolled across the frozen yard, melting the snow. Smoke rose high into the sky, black and curling. The snapping of pine needles catching on fire echoed through the air.

Watching the beautiful evergreens burn hurt Kaitlyn's heart. The only saving grace was the snow on the outer branches slowing the fire's progress. She prayed the fire didn't jump the perimeter fence and set off a forest fire across the mountain.

"I'll hold the hose while you turn the water on," Kaitlyn told him. Her numb hands struggled to grip the round rubber hose.

Soon a spray of water arched out of the end of the hose, hitting the trees. At least they could keep the cinders from reaching the house.

The sound of sirens brought a wave of relief cascading through her. Overhead, a forest service air tanker flew past, dropping water on the trees.

"Kaitlyn." Nick dropped the hose. "The fire department is here. They'll take care of the trees."

Large sprays of water arched over the tops of the trees from the other side of the fence, dousing the flames.

"Come on." Nick tugged at her. "We need to open the gate for the fire department. I need your help."

The plea grabbed her attention. She couldn't let him

go alone. She had to make sure the arsonists didn't make it onto the property.

She was surprised to see the paved driveway had been plowed. "Who did this?"

"Collin keeps the driveway clear," Nick replied as he ran beside her.

The cold air burned her lungs as she ran. At the large metal gate, Nick punched in a code. Kaitlyn slipped past the gate before it was fully open and met the fire chief and the sheriff where they were coordinating the effort to put out the fire.

"I didn't see what started the fire," she told them. "But it was on the backside of the fence."

The chief moved away to consult with his men.

"Kait," Nick called from the fire truck, waving. "I'm going with them."

His apparent glee at riding in a fire truck was apparent and so endearing. Despite the circumstances, she smiled and waved back.

Alex said, "Daniel is on horseback, riding along the outside fence to make sure there are no hidden fires. Or bad guys."

"I should be with him," she said as she tugged her phone from her pocket. "I could have my father bring my horse."

"Kaitlyn."

Alex's sharp tone froze her in place. "Sheriff?"

"Take a breath," he said, his expression softening. "You've done your part."

She wanted to do more. However, the unrelenting expression on his face made her acquiesce. With effort, she worked to calm her racing pulse as she watched the firefighters work. The urge to join in was strong, but she knew she'd only get in the firefighters' way.

Doing nothing chafed. Because she couldn't help with the fire or join Daniel, she paced, keeping a sharp eye out for any signs of the bad guys trying to worm their way past the gate.

Finally, the fire was out, and the chief came to report. "We found shards of glass and evidence of gasoline. I suspect a few Molotov cocktails were thrown over the fence. Despite the snow we've had, the trees ignited."

Arson, just as Kaitlyn had suspected.

Alex gave Kaitlyn a ride back to the house in his department-issued SUV. "Are you prepared to stay, or should I assign Chase or Daniel to take over for you?"

Weary, yet wired, Kaitlyn leaned her head back against the headrest. "I'm fine. I'm not going to let anything prevent me from doing my job."

Alex's approval shone in his eyes as he brought the SUV to a halt in front of the house. "Okay. I'll wait at the gate until it's closed before I head back to town."

"Thank you." She climbed out of the car and walked to the front door.

When she entered the house, Nick was waiting in the entryway for her. He was badly in need of a shower. Soot streaked his handsome face, and his hair stood on end. She could only imagine how horrible she looked. "Rosie?"

His tender gaze made Kaitlyn's insides turn to mush. "She's safe with Margaret and Collin."

Knowing everyone was safe allowed the adrenaline letdown to sweep through her, making her limbs shake. "Can you have Collin shut the gate after the sheriff?"

"I will do it," Nick said. "You look beat. We both need

to wash away the grime. We can meet in the library later. Take your time. You've earned it."

"The backyard is a mess," she said. "There's cleanup that needs to be done there."

"It can wait," he said, shooing her up the stairs.

Giving in to his suggestion, she nodded. Fatigue settled in her bones, making her steps heavy. She'd told Alex she wouldn't be run off this protection detail because she didn't want to let anyone down. Especially Nick and baby Rosie. Their lives were in her hands.

After a warm shower and change of clothes, Nick spent some time with Rosie before feeding her a bottle and putting her down for a late afternoon nap. He entered the library and found Kaitlyn sitting on the couch, barely able to keep her eyes open. The woman was a machine. At some point she was going to need to rest.

The sun, low in the sky, cast shadows through the room. He grabbed two bottles of water from the mini fridge in the corner.

"What made you decide to join your father and brother here in Bristle Township?" she asked, her voice soft, as if she didn't have the energy for more.

The question came out of the blue. Taking a seat next to her, he handed her a cool bottle of water. "Ian came to see me in New York after the house was completed to invite me for a visit." Nick twisted his lips. "Little did I realize he had an ulterior motive, but I shouldn't have been surprised."

"What did he want? I've always had the feeling Ian was more in charge than he let on."

Letting out a small, affection-filled laugh, Nick nodded. "You're not wrong. My big brother wanted for us to be a family again." He shook his head. "I thought maybe he'd sustained a head injury or something. But our father's health is declining, and Ian's determined that we have the remaining years with him together, as a family." With a shrug, he added, "I'd had no intention of sticking around for more than a few days when I first arrived."

Genuine curiosity brightened her gaze. "What made you stay?"

He stared at her for a moment. "The beauty of the mountains. The town and the people here."

Was that fond regard in her pretty eyes? Or maybe only a trick of the shadows.

Was she one of the reasons he'd stayed?

The question echoed through his brain.

Of course not. That would be ridiculous.

Still, the idea warmed him from the inside out. But he chose to keep that tidbit to himself. A little secret that maybe one day he'd share with her.

Kaitlyn couldn't shake the feeling that Nick was keeping something from her. Something important. But what, she couldn't guess.

Hearing Nick's reasons for staying in town was unexpected. She'd thought for sure he would tire of their small community a long time ago. But that was before Lexi Eng and her daughter arrived in Bristle Township with danger hot on their heels. Now Kaitlyn was beginning to see Nick in a different light. And she wasn't sure what to make of it.

Collin came into the library. "The Christmas tree delivery is here."

Kaitlyn's gut tightened. "That should be Trevor Howard."

"It could be a trick," Nick pointed out as he stood.

Collin winced. "You said to expect him."

"Yes, we did. And we are. But it doesn't hurt to be cautious," she said. "I'll go out front." Anxiety twisted in her chest. Would the bad guys try something so soon after their failed attempt to burn them out of the estate with the fire? She touched the grip of her holstered weapon.

"I'm coming with you," Nick said, dogging her heels to the front door.

Their coats were waiting on the marble table. Quickly donning the warm gear, they went outside and stood on the porch, listening. The smell of fire lingered despite the couple of hours since the flames had been extinguished.

Down the long driveway, the scraping of the large metal gate wheeling open echoed through the still air. They waited for the vehicle to traverse the half-mile drive. The sound of an engine grew closer and a blue pickup truck with a large Douglas fir tree strapped to the bed slowly made its way up the curvy drive toward the front porch steps.

Two people sat in the front cab.

Wariness knotted her shoulder muscles. "I told Trevor to come alone."

"He probably brought help, considering the size of that tree," Nick stated. "It's quite large. Maybe too large?"

The driver's-side visor was down, as was the passenger's.

The hairs at the base of her neck shook with warning. "I have a bad feeling about this. Go inside, Nick."

"I'm not leaving you here by yourself," he said.

As tempting as it was to school him on the fact that she was a deputy with a gun and didn't need his macho attitude, she kept her focus on the two people in the truck.

"Trevor?" she called out as she reached beneath her coat and rested her hand on her service weapon.

The two truck cab doors popped open, but neither of the occupants moved.

"Kaitlyn?" The concern in Nick's tone ratcheted up her own unease.

Removing her sidearm from the holster, she stepped in front of Nick. "Show me your hands," she yelled to the occupants of the truck.

The two men climbed out of the cab but turned so that their backs were facing Kaitlyn.

Uh-oh. The bad feeling that had taken hold of every muscle in her body turned into a full-blown storm of horrible. She nudged Nick as she stepped backward, keeping her weapon aimed at the truck. "Nick, inside. Now!"

In a coordinated move, both men whirled around, using the truck doors as shields, and leveled the barrels of automatic assault rifles at Kaitlyn.

Her heart stuttered to a stop. She and Nick were exposed and vulnerable.

"Put your weapon down, Deputy," the guy on the passenger's side shouted.

His knowledge that she was on duty, even though she wasn't in uniform, heightened Kaitlyn's tension even more. She couldn't see his face clearly, but the voice was familiar. The truth slammed into her brain. He was the thug who'd escaped from the hospital. That was how he knew she was with the sheriff's department.

Nick gripped Kaitlyn by the shoulders. Keeping herself in front of him, she allowed him to pull her toward the front door.

"What do you want?" she yelled to the two men.

"Hand over the flash drive," the driver said in a loud, booming voice.

"What's he talking about?" Nick asked softly.

Kaitlyn didn't have an answer.

"It's gotta be with the baby's stuff," the passenger yelled. "Bring us the baby and her stuff."

"Over my dead body. No way will I allow those goons to ever get their hands on Rosie," Nick muttered.

Afraid that would be exactly what would happen, Kaitlyn couldn't let Nick be harmed. The thought of something happening to him on her watch made her stomach drop and her mouth go dry. She swallowed back the bile churning in her gut to yell, "We searched everything. There is no flash drive."

Nick popped open the front door and yanked Kaitlyn backward into the house, slamming the door shut behind them.

The earsplitting sound of gunfire filled the air, and the noise shuddered through Kaitlyn. She dived over Nick. Collin crouched with his hands over his head. The pinging sound of bullets riddling the door, but not penetrating, brought Kaitlyn's head up. The firepower hadn't breached the door.

She rolled to the side and stared at Nick. "Armorplated front door?"

"Only the best for my father," he said as he sat up. "It's a good thing, no?"

"Yes. It is a very good thing. What about the front windows?"

Nick grinned. "Bulletproof. My father's paranoia is working in our favor."

Amazed by the security efforts put in place that she

hadn't known about, Kaitlyn sent up a prayer of thanksgiving. At the back of her mind, she wondered why Patrick Delaney was so paranoid that he'd build an impenetrable fortress. But her curiosity would have to wait.

Collin scuttled backward and disappeared into a back room.

Rosie's screams penetrated through the chaos of the gunfire. Nick's eyes widened and he jumped to his feet. He was moving toward the stairs as he said, "Rosie. I can't let anything happen to her."

Concern for the child's well-being burned in Kaitlyn's chest. "Grab her and get to the panic room," she called after him. "I'll take care of this."

She fumbled for her phone and dialed the sheriff's number. Putting the call on speaker, she crawled into the den that faced the front drive. The large plate-glass windows were pockmarked with bullet indentations. How long would the safety glass hold? The oversize couch provided excellent cover as she tried to see outside to assess what the assailants were up to.

The sheriff's voice came over the line. "Kaitlyn! The silent alarm for the estate went off."

"We're under attack. Armed men with AK-47s. Need backup."

"We're coming," came Alex's terse reply. "Keep this line open."

"Will do." She tucked the phone into her coat pocket.

Keeping low, she peered through an unmarred section of the window to see the two men had moved from behind the truck's doors and were walking toward the house, all the while indiscriminately peppering the front of the house with bullets.

Movement behind the truck caught her attention. A

dark sedan raced up the drive at a fast speed. It stopped about twenty feet from the rear of the truck. More bad guys?

Where was Trevor?

Kaitlyn gritted her teeth and sent up a quick prayer that backup would arrive before the men found a way inside the house.

SEVEN

The sedan's driver's-side door was flung open, and a man who had short light brown hair and was wearing a navy wool peacoat and dress slacks jumped out. Friend or foe? He looked too well dressed to be a thug. Interesting. Kaitlyn tensed, waiting to see what he would do.

In a crouch, he ran to the back of the truck, drawing a handgun from an underarm holster as he went. Using the truck as a shield, he aimed and fired. Not at the house, but at the men from the truck, wounding the driver in the leg. The driver went down.

Stunned by this turn of events, Kaitlyn ran to the front door and eased it open to take advantage of the opportunity created by the new arrival. She aimed and fired at the second gunman, the one from the hospital. The goon jerked, losing his hold on the assault rifle, sending it sliding beneath the truck. Her bullet had winged him. Grabbing his now bleeding arm, he fled back to the truck, dived into the cab and started the engine. The vehicle reversed, backing into the sedan.

The well-dressed man jumped out of the way as the would-be Christmas tree protruding from the truck bed crashed through the sedan's front window. The sedan was pushed backward as the truck continued in reverse. Then the gunman driving the truck turned the truck, tree and sedan in an arc. The tree broke with a loud *crack*, its top half firmly wedged through the front windshield of the sedan. Released, the truck peeled across the snow-covered lawn. Throwing dirt, sod and snow in its wake, the truck sped down the drive toward the open gate.

Kaitlyn clenched her jaw in frustration that one of the gunmen was getting away. But the other wasn't going anywhere, was still writhing on the ground and clutching at his wounded leg.

The newcomer advanced on the man he'd shot and kicked the assault rifle away. He quickly holstered his weapon. Then he crouched down to flip the injured man onto his stomach and zip-tie his wrists together.

Obviously, he was some sort of law enforcement, but Kaitlyn had never seen this man before and wasn't about to trust him. Cautiously, she moved closer, keeping her gun trained on him. "Identify yourself."

The man rose and held up his hands. "I'm going to reach for my ID." Slowly, he reached inside his jacket pocket and produced a black leather credentials wallet.

Kaitlyn took the leather case and inspected the identification. *FBI* was embossed on it in big blue letters, and there was a photo of Special Agent Jim Porter that matched the man standing before her. The ID looked legitimate.

Kaitlyn stared at him for a long moment, remembering the last time a stranger had come into town claiming to be a member of law enforcement. The man had actually been an assassin sent to kill Kaitlyn's friend Ashley Willis. "How do I know this is real?"

"At the moment, you're just going to have to trust me," Porter said.

"Not likely," she said. "Keep your hands in the air."

The distant wail of a siren let Kaitlyn know the sheriff was close. Keeping her weapon aimed at the men in front of her with one hand, she used the other to dig out her phone, still connected to Alex's phone, from her coat pocket and told him what had happened. "Be on the lookout for the Howards' blue truck with half a tree in its bed. The guy driving is the gunman from the hospital. I wounded him this time."

"Yeah, the truck just passed us," Alex said. "I'll have Daniel intercept."

"You need to find Trevor Howard," she said. "He might be injured." She lifted a prayer that he wasn't dead. She'd known him and his family her entire life. It would devastate the community of Bristle Township to lose one of their own.

"I'll put a call out to the mounted patrol," he promised. "We'll find him. An ambulance is right behind us."

"We have another situation." She told him about the FBI agent.

"Keep an eye on him," Alex said. "We'll be there in minutes."

"He's not going anywhere," she said and tucked the phone back into her jacket pocket.

"If you don't want this guy to bleed out," Porter said, "I suggest compression on his wound."

He was right. They needed this guy alive and talking.

"Stay there," she told Porter. She backed up the concrete steps to the front door. "Collin," she yelled through the opening.

"Yes, ma'am?" came his reply from somewhere deep in the bowels of the house.

"I need clean towels. We have a wounded man out here."

"We already called 911," Margaret yelled. "Is it safe?"

"Yes, it's safe." Kaitlyn chanced a glance up the staircase and shouted, "Nick?"

A few seconds later, Nick appeared at the top of the stairs. He appeared unharmed. The knot in Kaitlyn's chest loosened.

"Are you okay, Kaitlyn?"

"I'm good. You? Rosie?" She kept her eyes and her weapon on Porter.

"We're fine. She's with Margaret and Collin." Nick hurried to her side and stared past Kaitlyn. "Who is that?"

"Claims to be FBI."

Collin came out of the house with a handful of clean towels.

Agent Porter took the towels and pressed them against the wounded man's leg. "If you want to live, hold these in place," he told the man, who nodded and did as instructed.

The sound of the siren grew louder as Alex's SUV skidded to a halt a few feet from them. Sheriff Alex Trevino and Deputy Chase Fredrick jumped out; both men had their weapons drawn. Kaitlyn gave the FBI agent and the suspect a wide berth to hand her boss Agent Porter's credentials.

"Looks legit, but we'll see." Alex handed the leather holder off to Chase. "Call the local FBI in Denver. See if this is one of their agents."

Chase hurried away.

"I'm not with the Denver office," Porter said. "I work out of DC."

"You're a long way from home," Alex said.

"I'm working a case. My informant was headed here. Lexi Eng."

Kaitlyn's surprise mirrored Nick's as they shared a glance.

Porter's gaze went to Nick. "Rosie is Lexi's baby, right? Are Lexi and her baby here?"

"What do you want with Lexi?" Nick asked.

"It's classified. Strictly need to know," Porter said. "I need to speak with Lexi. Now. Where is she?"

"We're not answering any of your questions," Alex said. "Until we've confirmed your identity."

Chase jogged back. "He's FBI with the Washington, DC, office. They gave me the runaround, though. They wouldn't tell me what case he's working on."

Everyone looked at Agent Porter.

He shrugged. "Like I said, it's classified. Let me talk to Lexi."

Kaitlyn turned her gaze to Nick. What had his friend been mixed up in? Whatever it was put the people of Bristle Township in jeopardy. Something she just wouldn't allow.

"She's in the hospital fighting for her life," Nick said, his voice vibrating with the anger crowding his chest.

There was no mistaking the shock in Porter's brown eyes. "Is she alive?"

Nick nodded. "Barely. But some guys tried to kill her. Do you know who?" He flicked his gaze at the man being treated by the paramedics who had arrived a few minutes after the sheriff. "Who do they work for? They keep asking about a flash drive. What's on it?"

"Did you find it?" Porter asked. The intensity in his eyes burned bright.

Nick shook his head, frustrated that the agent wasn't giving them any information.

"You said she's your informant," Kaitlyn said. "What's going on? What is your case about?"

"I have to go to the hospital." Porter turned to Alex. "Sheriff, can you give me a ride, since my car is toast?"

"We'll give you a ride to town," Alex said. "But you will not go anywhere near our assault victim. We don't want anything to impede her recovery."

Nick didn't like the situation at all, and he didn't trust this man. Why wouldn't he tell them what was going on? What was Lexi involved in? Nick thought about the necklace he'd found in the diaper bag. It was just a trinket, nothing special, certainly nothing worth all this fuss. And not a flash drive. Or was it...? Could the little butterfly charm hold a USB drive?

Nick was not about to reveal anything to the FBI agent because he didn't know the man's agenda. If Porter were trustworthy, why hadn't Lexi run to him? Nick kept quiet about the necklace and instead asked Agent Porter, "What can you tell us about Rosie?"

The agent's gaze focused intently on Nick. "All I know is she's Lexi's child."

Nick didn't buy it. The man knew more than he was saying. "Who was Lexi involved with?"

"I cannot give you any information regarding Lexi Eng. It's all classified. Way above any of your pay grades." Agent Porter turned back to Alex. "Sheriff, that ride into town?"

Alex narrowed his gaze. "Hmmm." He turned to Chase. "Let's go." He glanced back at Kaitlyn. "Keep in touch."

"Yes, sir," she said.

Alex, Chase and Agent Porter left in the sheriff's vehicle. Once the gate closed behind the SUV, Kaitlyn turned to Nick. "Classified, my eye. I don't trust him."

"Me, either."

"Did you see the look on his face when you asked him about Rosie?" Kaitlyn asked. "Do you think he could be Rosie's father?"

"Could Lexi have been running from this agent?" Nick's heart tumbled. "If so, then I told Porter where to find her. Is he the one behind the attacks? Did he shoot his own man?"

"I'll text Alex our concern and double-check that they keep Agent Porter from going to the hospital," Kaitlyn stated.

"Thank you," Nick said as they headed back inside.

"I wonder what's on the flash drive that is important enough to make these men willing to kill for it. And why does the FBI want it?" Kaitlyn mused.

"Something illegal." His gut twisted with certainty. Why would Lexi get involved in criminal activity? The woman he'd known three years ago had been sweet, hardworking and full of plans for her future. What had happened to her?

"There was nothing at the crash site," Kaitlyn said. "One of the goons said the flash drive would be with the baby, but we checked the car seat and diaper bag. Nothing." She shrugged out of her coat. "We have to find that flash drive before anyone else gets hurt."

Nick couldn't stay quiet any longer. It felt too much

like lying. One thing he wouldn't do to Kaitlyn. "I did find something in Rosie's diaper bag."

Kaitlyn faced him, her eyebrows raised and her eyes sparking. "And you're just now telling me this?"

He met her gaze. "I didn't think it was anything important. It's just a trinket. A child's necklace with rhinestones. Not worth anything."

"You let me be the judge of that."

Faced with her anger, he realized he should have told her the moment he'd found it. He was already aware she didn't trust easily. And now the rocky ground he stood on could become an avalanche.

Nick sighed with regret. "I'm sorry, Kait. I honestly didn't think the piece of costume jewelry was worth mentioning."

Her lips pressed into a thin line. "Where is this necklace?"

"I'll show you." He led the way upstairs. In the nursery, he went to the crib and unhooked the butterfly necklace from the mobile.

He offered the trinket to Kaitlyn, who took it, frowning.

"Okay," she said. "I can see why you wouldn't think this to be anything worthwhile. It's a child's piece of cheap jewelry."

"That's what I thought." Nick put out his hand again. "May I?"

Kaitlyn handed it back to him.

He inspected the charm. On the back there was a faint but definite line. Could it be a hinge? His heart rate ticked up. He grasped both of the butterfly's wings and bent it until it came apart. He held up the two pieces. One side was a small flash drive.

"Not so worthless after all," Kaitlyn murmured. "That is clever."

Nick handed it over for her to inspect.

"Do you have a computer?" Kaitlyn asked.

"I do. In here." Nick opened the door to his bedroom and flipped on the light. He walked to the desk situated in the corner where his laptop sat. Kaitlyn followed him.

Nick glanced at Kaitlyn. Her curious gaze bounced around the room. When she met his gaze, he was sure her cheeks were turning pink. He ignored the thrill of knowing that being in his inner sanctuary flustered her as he sat in the chair facing the computer. She handed him the flash drive. He plugged the tiny butterfly wing into the USB port. A window popped up but a password was to unlock the drive.

"Any ideas?" she asked.

"No. I don't know Lexi well enough to make a guess what her password would be."

"Yet she came to you for help…" she mused. "Try Rosie's name."

Nick typed it in. The window shimmied and the box turned red, indicating the wrong password.

"Try Rosie's birth date," Kaitlyn directed.

Confused, he looked up at Kaitlyn. "We don't know Rosie's birthday."

She patted his shoulder. "Yes, we do. It was on the birth certificate."

Shaking his head at his own folly, Nick said, "Of course. How could I forget?"

He typed in the date he recalled from the fake birth certificate that claimed him as Rosie's father. The date unlocked the drive, but the file that came up was encrypted. "I don't have anything on my laptop that would be able to crack this code."

"I'm sure Hannah does," Kaitlyn said. "The department's forensic specialist and computer tech is our best option."

"Yes, I imagine she would be," Nick agreed. He liked the redheaded woman, but he wasn't attracted to her the way he was to Kaitlyn.

"Can you click out of this?" Kaitlyn asked.

Nick ejected the flash drive.

Kaitlyn put the two pieces of the necklace back together. "I'll hang on to this. I need to call Alex."

Afraid that whatever was on the flash drive would cause Lexi and Rosie more harm, Nick said, "We can't give it to the FBI agent until we know what's on it."

"If he's legit, we have to tell him about this," Kaitlyn said.

Nick smiled grimly to himself. Always the rule follower. That was his Kaitlyn.

His pulse jumped. When did he start thinking of her as *his*? Ridiculous. But for now she was under his protection as long as she was under his roof. A position he'd never expected or realized he wanted. And even though, technically, she was here to protect him and Rosie, he wanted to keep Kaitlyn safe. So, in essence, they were protecting each other. However, he highly doubted Kaitlyn would think he could do anything to protect her. "Will Alex make sure that Agent Porter isn't the one behind this?"

Confidence firmed Kaitlyn's jaw. "I know Alex will check the guy out. Even if he has to rattle every cage possible."

"Good."

She stepped out of the room to make the call. Nick checked on Rosie. The baby had fallen back to sleep. Being awoken by all the chaos of alarms and gunfire couldn't have been good for her. Nick wished he could foresee other potential hazards but, unfortunately, he couldn't. He lifted a prayer that God would continue to protect them.

After securing the blanket around Rosie, Nick left the nursery and joined Kaitlyn in the hallway.

"I left a message for Alex to call me back," she said.

Carrying the baby monitor with him, Nick said, "All this drama has left me feeling quite famished."

Kaitlyn shook her head with humor sparking in her eyes. "You're such a guy."

"Glad you noticed," he quipped with a grin. If only she thought of him as a man she could see herself spending time with that didn't include flying bullets.

Her phone rang as they descended the staircase. "Hey, Chase." She listened, then said, "That's good to know. Thank you for telling me. Is Alex around? Oh, okay. I left him a message."

After hanging up, she said to Nick, "They found Trevor Howard. He'd been left bound and gagged on the side of the road leading to the estate. According to Trevor, two men jumped him as he left the tree farm and held him at gunpoint until they got to a remote spot on the side of the road leading here. He managed to roll out from behind the bushes where the two thugs had stashed him. Chase said he's unharmed but shaken."

Nick let out a relieved breath. "Praise God."

With a nod of agreement, she continued, "Trevor had seen the two men around town the past few days, but he wasn't exactly sure how they knew about him delivering the tree."

"Someone must have heard him talking to you," Nick said.

"Or Trevor could have mentioned it to someone and that someone mentioned it to someone else and so on. One of the many pitfalls of a small community," Kaitlyn said. "News of any kind spreads like wildfire."

Worry churned in his gut. "Do you think people are discussing you being here?" He wouldn't want her reputation tarnished on his account.

She rolled her eyes. "I'm doing my job. If anyone thinks differently, that's their problem."

He knew firsthand how public perception and reality could differ, as well as the damage the divide between the two could cause. He hoped Kaitlyn wouldn't suffer any backlash because of him. The last thing he ever wanted to do was hurt this woman who'd become so important to him. Important enough that he needed to find a way to release her from this duty.

Tomorrow he'd talk to the sheriff about having someone else assigned to Rosie's protection until the Trent Associates people could arrive. It would be the right thing to do.

And the hardest.

Of course, once they discovered the contents of the flash drive, there wouldn't be a need for protection. Or spending time with Kaitlyn.

The thought was depressing.

EIGHT

Later that night, too restless to sleep, Kaitlyn found Nick in the dining room with the unboxed Christmas decorations.

"Need help?" she asked.

"I'd love some help," he said. "I was going stir-crazy in my room."

Nodding in understanding, she opened a box. They laid out the ornaments on a thick blanket Nick had spread over the large dining room table in anticipation of the Christmas tree that would eventually be delivered and set up in front of the large windows at her back.

She was amazed at the collection of ornaments. Many were pieces of artwork that shouldn't be hung on a tree but rather displayed in a museum. She unwrapped a beautiful, hollowed-out eggshell hand-painted with a forest motif and with a hole carved out of the middle. Inside, a tiny wooden deer figurine stood beside her fawn.

She held it up and marveled. "This is incredible."

Nick glanced at the ornament dangling from the red ribbon. "I believe that came from a trip my parents took to Prague. My mother loved to collect decorations from their travels."

Laying the delicate piece on the table, she said, "It's a nice tradition."

"I suppose you're right," Nick said as he laid down a wooden crab with State of Maine written across it.

The trill of Kaitlyn's cell phone, muted by her jeans pocket, had her scrambling to answer. The caller ID said it was the sheriff's department. This would be a good time to tell Alex about finding the flash drive hidden in the butterfly necklace.

"Alex, I'm glad you called. There's some—"

"Kaitlyn, I have sad news about Lexi," he said, cutting her off.

Her breath stalled in her lungs. "I'm here with Nick and putting you on speakerphone."

"Nick, I'm sorry to say that Lexi Eng succumbed to her injuries and passed away a half hour ago. We've officially ruled her death a homicide."

Sorrow speared Kaitlyn for a life cut short too soon. Poor Rosie was now without a mother. It was even more imperative that Kaitlyn find the baby's father.

Nick wobbled as if his legs could no longer keep him upright. The color had drained from his face. Kaitlyn grasped his elbow. "You should sit and put your head between your knees."

He shrugged off her hand. "I'm fine." He moved to stand in front of the windows overlooking the valley below.

Kaitlyn ached with empathy for him. He cared for Lexi, and now his friend was dead.

Keeping a hand on Nick's shoulder, Kaitlyn spoke into the phone. "What did you learn about Agent Porter? Did he visit Lexi? Could he have…?" Her stomach knotted. Was the agent behind Lexi's accident and death?

"Porter did not see Lexi," Alex stated firmly. "I've had hospital security, as well as a deputy, standing guard at her door. The doctor said they couldn't stop the internal bleeding."

Kaitlyn prayed Lexi hadn't been in pain.

"I rattled cages on the state level," Alex continued. "Both the governor and the seated senator of Colorado are putting out feelers to learn what they can on Porter and the case he's working. Hopefully, I'll know more tomorrow."

"I have news, as well," she said. "Nick re-searched Rosie's diaper bag and found a pendant that is actually a USB flash drive."

"That is big news. What's on it?"

"The file is encrypted," she told him. "I know Hannah could decipher the encryption. Now that we have the flash drive, Rosie and Nick should be out of danger, don't you think?"

"Until we know what's on the drive, you need to stay with them," Alex said. "In the morning I'll have Daniel or Chase drive out to pick it up."

"All right."

"Nick, I'm sorry about Lexi," Alex said.

Nick glanced over his shoulder. "Thank you, Alex."

After saying goodbye and hanging up, Kaitlyn moved to stand next to Nick. The view of Bristle Township and the county was stunning and took her breath away once again. The many lights of the residences glistened like little diamonds on black velvet. She took Nick's hand and laced her fingers through his.

If the circumstances were different, she'd find this very romantic. But someone had just died, and the persons responsible were still at large.

When Nick faced her, his eyes were red rimmed and angry. "Why did she have to die? She was so young," he said. "What was she involved in? Why would she risk leaving her child? Now Rosie will grow up without her mother." He shook his head, his lips tightening into a thin line.

Kaitlyn's heart ached for him. He'd lost his mother at a young age. That had to have been difficult. "Rosie is safe, and she has you," Kaitlyn said. "You're taking great care of her and you will continue to until other arrangements are made."

Nick straightened. "No other arrangements need to be made. She will have everything she needs and everything she deserves. And more. With me."

Kaitlyn knew what she had to say, even though the words were heavy on her tongue. "Nick, I have to find her father."

Pain crossed Nick's face. He opened his mouth, no doubt to argue with her, but then he heaved a sigh. "I know. It's the right thing to do. And you always do the right thing."

She frowned, not sure his words were a compliment. "Going outside the lines of what's right is wrong. It's that simple."

"But there's a reason Lexi put my name down on the certificate. You have to keep that in mind." Nick stared her in the eye. "If Rosie's father is a bad man, you cannot give Rosie to him."

"If Rosie's biological father is a bad man, you can be sure I will do everything I can to prove he's not fit for custody. But it's not my call. A judge will determine what is in the best interest of Rosie."

"Staying here with me is in her best interest," he insisted.

She wanted to comfort him, promise him that he'd never lose Rosie, but she couldn't. Even if she couldn't find Rosie's biological father, would a judge deem Nick fit as an adoptive parent? She cringed. His reputation didn't exactly bolster confidence. "Nick, you have to be realistic. You have a record."

He blinked. "You did a background check on me?"

She wouldn't apologize for doing her job. "Yes. When your father launched the treasure hunt, we needed to know who we were dealing with."

"I see." Nick's lips twisted. "So whatever is in my file means that's who I am. No wonder you—" He shook his head. "A person isn't the sum of a report. There's always more to the story."

She knew that all too well. "Then tell me your story. Explain to me why you were arrested several times."

"Arrested, but never charged," he shot back. He visibly swallowed. "Come," he said, pulling her into the library, where they sat down on the leather sofa in front of the window that was riddled with pockmarks, reminding Kaitlyn how close they'd come to losing their lives.

She made a mental note to talk to Nick about replacing the window and door, but it would have to wait. She wanted to hear his version of the events that had led to his being arrested multiple times. She had to admit to herself that reading those reports had colored her opinion of Nick. Her mother was always lamenting that she saw the world only in black and white and never shades of gray. But being a cop shaped her view of life. She only knew what she could prove for herself. Which had made believing in God difficult, but somehow, He had softened her heart enough for her to accept Jesus. Accepting others was still a trial.

Over the past few days she'd come to realize she'd misjudged Nick on many levels. Though it was difficult for her, she needed to keep an open mind.

"I've already told you that my mother was fragile."

Kaitlyn nodded, but refrained from asking what his mother's health had to do with his police record.

He made a face, then straightened his spine and shoulders. "She loved her children."

His words sounded wooden and rehearsed, as if he'd repeated them often. Kaitlyn's heart squeezed tight. Had he doubted his mother's love?

"She did her best." He seemed to slump slightly. "After the many nannies who came and went, Ian and I were sent away to boarding school. I was eight."

Kaitlyn's breath hitched. "You came home on holidays, right?"

"Not always. Boarding school was year-round. At first, Ian and I were sent to the same school." Nick's shoulders lifted, then fell. "We had each other. But then he was sent on to a different school. And I was left alone."

"That's rough." She thought back to her own childhood. It had been idyllic in many ways, with two parents who loved her and each other, and she'd had horses as her companions.

His lips twisted. "I was angry. Hurt. I lashed out a lot, mostly verbally."

Sympathy wove through her. She could only imagine how his young boy's heart had felt abandoned.

"We're not too different, you and I," he said.

She frowned slightly, having just thought how different their childhoods had been. "Really? How so?"

"You work to bring justice for those who need it. Only you do it in ways that society accepts. Me, I sought justice in less accepted ways. It only got me in trouble. But I could handle it as long as those who were being hurt were left alone."

Kaitlyn turned his words over and over in her head. "I don't understand."

"I was always in trouble for fighting, mostly. I can't abide bullies."

A sentiment she understood and shared. "So you... did what?"

"One day I saw a bigger kid picking on a smaller one and I lost it." He gave her a lazy grin. "I got in between them. The bully thought he could take me on." Nick laughed softly. "Little did he know, even though I was small myself, I'd had some training."

"Training?"

"One of our many nannies had a brother who was into mixed martial arts. He taught Ian and I some grappling and striking techniques. Enough that we could defend ourselves if we were ever grabbed. I'm pretty sure my father arranged for the lessons. Back then he was concerned that one of us would be kidnapped."

Kaitlyn nodded. "I'm sure being from a rich shipping family would attract some unsavory attention. That explains the security measures."

"The shipping company is only one of many endeavors that my father, and grandfather before him, engaged in that made our family targets. The most recent being the treasure hunt. But those men who shot up the front of the house had nothing to do with my father or the family businesses."

"True." This present danger had come from Lexi. Directing the conversation back to the matter at hand, she prompted, "The bully. You beat him up?"

"I bloodied his nose and blackened his eye. But, apparently, I should have told a teacher instead. I didn't last long at that school." He stretched his legs. "And so it went at every school I attended. When I tried to explain that the person I was fighting with had been bullying the weaker kids, I was not believed. Nor was I believed when I did go to the school admin about a teacher who was abusing his students."

Empathy cramped Kaitlyn's chest. Her blood pounded in her ears as the old wound knocked at her mind, wanting to be let out of its box.

"I was kicked out of one boarding school after another," Nick continued. "After a while, I stopped trying to explain. But I made it known at every school I attended that if I ever heard of students being bullied, I would come back. And I did return to a couple of schools that I'd been expelled from as a reminder that bullies wouldn't be tolerated, which accounts for the arrests. I was considered persona non grata. But my father had good lawyers on retainer, and I was a juvenile. At least, for most of the arrests. It was trickier when I turned eighteen. Still, I was charged, but the charges were later dropped. By then, I had discovered that money had more power than my might. Many of the schools realized stricter non-bullying policies came with hefty donations."

Kaitlyn was reeling. She didn't quite know how to process what he was telling her. The fact that he'd stood up for his classmates who were being bullied made her respect him in surprising ways. And brought back horrible memories of her own. Tears pricked her eyes. Despite her best efforts, her vision swam with the increasing moisture until she couldn't contain it anymore.

"Kaitlyn?"

She vehemently wiped at the tears streaking down her cheeks, doing her best to stem the flow. Why was she letting his story dredge up her own horrible nightmare?

"What is it?" Nick took her hand this time, his fingers curling over her fingers, his palm pressed flat against hers, which was both reassuring and unnerving.

"It's nothing." She tugged at her hand, but he refused to release her.

"It is something," he said. "My story shouldn't upset you this badly."

"I know what it's like to not be believed when unjustly accused of something." She cringed at the admission.

His eyes widened. "Please, tell me."

A heaviness descended onto her shoulders. The words stuck in her throat; taking a breath became difficult. "I—I can't."

He arched an eyebrow. "Is it classified?"

She pushed out a small laugh in spite of the dread gripping her chest. "No, it's not classified. It's just very personal and very painful."

Even saying that made her feel vulnerable, and she didn't like being vulnerable or helpless. Her foot bounced as panicky energy coursed through her veins. Anxiety twisted along her nerve endings. She recognized the sensations, ones she'd long thought she had under control, but here she was, on the verge of a panic attack with Nick as a witness. She had to get herself under control. She didn't want him to see her as weak. Ever.

"Pastor Brown once told me," Nick said softly, his voice soothing as he held her gaze, "fear holds us in prison to keep us from God's love. And the only way to break out is to look that fear in the eye and say *I will not be afraid.*"

Her mouth dried.

He continued, "Did you know that the Bible says *fear not* nearly eighty times?" Nick squeezed her hand. "God wants us to hear His message. With God, we don't have to be imprisoned by fear."

She stared at him, her mind grappling with Nick's wise words. Yes, he was repeating what he'd been told by Pastor Brown, but Nick had internalized the message.

Try as she might, she couldn't bring herself to tell him about what had happened to her. He was her assignment, not her confidant. It wouldn't be professional for her to talk to him about her past.

She dried her tears and stood, forcing him to let go of her hand. "Thank you for sharing the truth about your police record. What you did was wrong in the eyes of the law. You should never take justice into your own hands, but I believe your intentions weren't criminal. You are more than a file, Nick. Much, much more."

Nick sat on the couch and watched Kaitlyn hurry out of the library. His heart sank. How could he help her? She was so full of distrust that he ached for her. He'd always thought it was just him, that he rubbed her the wrong way. But now he recognized that her distrust stemmed from something else. His story had triggered some painful memory in her past.

He didn't regret revealing the true reason he'd been in trouble so much as a youth. But he did feel bad that he'd caused her pain. He never wanted to intentionally hurt this woman.

Heeding an inner nudging to go after her, to not let her continue to stay frozen in fear, he rose from the couch and hurried out of the library. He caught up with her before she could take the stairs. He threaded his fingers through hers again, liking the feel of her capable hand in his. "Kaitlyn, please, don't run away from me."

Slowly, she turned to face him. Her stoic expression made his heart tumble. This fierce, independent, strong woman was struggling so hard not to allow any vulnerability to show. He couldn't resist the need to take her in his arms. He fully expected her to resist, but she came into his embrace, though her body was tense and wooden. He rubbed little circles on her back until she finally melted against him. Everything inside of him sighed with tenderness that she would allow him to offer a bit of solace.

"I'm sorry, Kaitlyn, for whatever happened to you."

She shook her head against his shoulder. "It has nothing to do with you."

"But it does," he said. "It's keeping you from trusting me."

She pulled back to look into his eyes. Her right hand rested over his heart. His pulse spiked. Her touch was electrifying, but the emotions welling up inside were unfamiliar, terrifying and exhilarating. If he wasn't careful, he could fall hard for this woman.

"You are a good man, Nick Delaney."

His chest expanded with affection and pride. "Then talk to me."

"You are also persistent."

He couldn't help but grin. "It's a Delaney trait."

Her mouth softened. Her lips beckoned. He wanted to kiss her with every fiber of his being. But he instinctively recognized that giving in to the yearning would most likely send her scuttling away from him like a scared rabbit. He didn't want her to be scared. Not of him. "It's okay," he said. "You don't have to tell me."

She bit her bottom lip, once again drawing his gaze. "Maybe I will someday. But I can't right now. Not yet."

Her gaze dropped from his eyes to his lips. He swallowed, his throat as parched as if he were in a desert. He needed to retreat now, before he changed his mind and gave in to the yearning to sweep her off her feet.

Who was he kidding? She wasn't a woman who would allow herself to be swept away. When, and if, she gave her heart away, it would be by her choice.

And he couldn't envision a scenario where he'd ever be so blessed that she might choose him.

NINE

Kaitlyn paced the yellow bedroom. Early morning sunlight, made more intense by the reflection off the snow covering the ground and trees, filtered through the gauzy curtains. She'd been dressed in civilian clothes, jeans and a fresh sweater, for hours and ready to get the day started but hadn't heard Nick leave his room or a peep from the baby.

So she waited. And paced.

The knot in her stomach tightened with each step. All night she'd wrestled with the fact that Nick wasn't the degenerate man she'd once thought him to be. Her mind was blown.

Why did learning Nick was a champion for the underdog make him so much more appealing?

She'd already been struggling with her unwanted attraction to the man. Now, learning he was actually a good guy… No, that wasn't fair to him. He'd always been a good guy; she just hadn't wanted to acknowledge it.

Why?

Because she'd built him up to be just like Jason.

She put a hand to her forehead in regret for not being brave enough to talk to Nick about her painful history with her college crush. Just thinking about Jason brought back the feelings of helplessness and vulnerability that she'd vowed never to allow herself to experience again. Telling Nick about that awful time would only make her weak in his eyes and give him power over her. And she couldn't permit that.

A light knock on her door froze her in place. Steadying her breathing, she opened the door to find Nick standing there holding Rosie, looking so cute together her heart ached.

Nick wore khaki pants and a long-sleeve Henley shirt in an amber color that complemented the tone of his skin. Rosie wore a sweet knit hat over her dark smattering of hair, and her chubby cheeks beckoned for a kiss. Kaitlyn had never felt the urge to kiss a baby before. What was that about?

"Everything okay?" Nick asked. "You're frowning."

Intentionally clearing her expression, she said, "I'm surprised to see you both up so early. It's only six a.m."

Wagging his eyebrows, Nick said, "I don't think Rosie cares much about time."

"I didn't hear her cry," Kaitlyn said. Or him leave his room. She must have really been wallowing too deep in her head. Not good. Or professional. Definitely time to get back to the station and her job of protecting the whole town, not just one handsome man and an adorable baby. Back to where she was safe. At least emotionally. She needed to talk to the sheriff.

"I got to her before she could cry out," he said and nuzzled Rosie.

The tender expression on his face made Kaitlyn's insides melt and at the same time stirred an unfamiliar yearning deep in her core. He really had fallen in love with the baby. What would it be like to have him look at her with such tender regard? With love?

She swallowed back the panic the thought generated. She wasn't interested in falling in love. Or having Nick love her.

Because... All her old excuses for holding him at bay had disintegrated last night, leaving only an uncomfortable, hollow space. She straightened her spine against the emptiness.

"Breakfast should be ready soon," Nick said, forcing her to regroup and refocus. "Are you hungry?"

Before she could respond, the chime of her cell phone sounded. "I'll be right there."

Nick nodded and walked downstairs.

Kaitlyn closed the door and grabbed her phone off the charger. The caller ID let her know it was the sheriff. "Alex?"

"Hey. Busy morning here. I can't spare anyone to come get the flash drive. You'll need to keep custody of it until one of us can get there," Alex said. "I'd send Hannah, but she's overloaded right now with processing the scene."

Her stomach clenched. She needed to be back on duty, helping to keep the town safe. "What's happening?"

"There's been an accident on the highway into town. I've sent Daniel and Chase out to deal with it. I'm holding down the fort here. The Christmas celebrations are bringing in lots of tourists, and that always requires some monitoring even when we don't have armed men in town looking for some mysterious flash drive."

"We really do need to hire another deputy," she said. With Alex taking on the sheriff's position, the department was left one deputy short.

"I've assembled the mounted patrol," he said. "They will take turns keeping the peace on horseback in town during the sidewalk craft fair this afternoon and during the Christmas parade this weekend. After the New Year, I'll start searching for someone to fill the job."

She liked how methodically and strategically Alex operated. He was the right person to be the new sheriff. "Any new developments with the Feds?"

"Nothing so far. I'll let you know the minute there are."

"Fair enough."

"I'll talk to you soon." Alex hung up.

Kaitlyn headed downstairs and followed the sound of voices coming from the kitchen. She found Nick, Rosie, Margaret and Collin gathered around the counter. Nick was eating a stack of pancakes while bouncing Rosie on his knee. He was really getting the hang of parenting.

"Have a seat, Deputy," Margaret said as she put a plate piled with fluffy pancakes on the table in front of a vacant seat.

"Thank you." Kaitlyn sat and poured warmed syrup over the pancakes. "You're the best, Margaret."

The woman smiled with appreciation, then gave her husband a look.

"If you need anything, just ring," Collin said as he and Margaret made a hasty exit.

Kaitlyn watched them leave. What had sent them scurrying out? Surely they hadn't left the room to give her and Nick "alone" time.

Nick smiled, his dark brown eyes soft as he met her gaze. "You're looking fierce again. Did the sheriff have news about Agent Porter?"

"Not yet." She set her fork down. "The department

is spread thin. No one's available to come get the flash drive and take it to Hannah."

"You can take the flash drive into town," he said.

"I can't leave you all here unprotected." As much as she wanted to get back to her customary duties as a deputy, she wasn't going to leave Nick and Rosie vulnerable to attack.

"I arranged for some extra security measures after yesterday," Nick said. "There shouldn't be a problem with you leaving."

Surprise washed through her. "Like what?"

"More cameras and motion sensors set up along the road leading to the main gate," he said. "A crew came late last night and installed them. They were able to remotely patch the feed to the monitors we have here. The windows and door will be replaced later this week."

"Good thinking on the cameras and motion sensors," she said.

"Also, the private protection company I contacted called this morning, and they have sent operatives. I'm expecting them anytime now."

She blinked, a bit stunned and for some odd reason disappointed that her replacements would be arriving soon. She should be glad. It was time for this assignment to be over. Time for her to leave the Delaney estate. Despite how massive the house and grounds were, there was a confining aspect to being here. She couldn't roam off for some quiet time; she needed to stay close to Rosie. To Nick. And that was messing with her, bigtime. "I should stay to vet the security people."

He tilted his head and studied her. "Okay. I would appreciate that. And then I'll head to town with you."

Kaitlyn shook her head. "There's no need for you to leave."

"I have to make arrangements for Lexi. There's paperwork that I'll need to sign," he said.

Understanding engulfed her. Of course, he would take on the responsibility of seeing to funeral arrangements for Rosie's mother. He was that kind of guy. A guy people could count on. Kaitlyn had to admit he was a guy she could count on. But she didn't want to fall for this man. The quicker she returned to her normal routine, the better. "What about Rosie?"

"She'll be in good hands with Margaret and Collin." He shook his head. "Those two. They've taken to being surrogate grandparents like ducks to water."

"I've noticed." She was glad for Rosie's sake.

The distinct roar of a helicopter's rotor blades echoed through the house. The bird was closing in fast.

"Good timing," Nick said. "That must be the Trent people now."

Margaret and Collin returned to the kitchen.

"I'll take Rosie upstairs and check her diaper." Margaret held out her arms. Nick transferred Rosie to her. Then Margaret left the kitchen, humming to the baby.

Collin handed them each their coats, then gave Nick some papers. "This is the verification code to confirm the identity of the new protection detail."

Donning her coat, Kaitlyn told herself it was a good thing to have bodyguards here. Now there was no reason she would have to come back or spend any more time with Nick. Why that thought upset her, she couldn't fathom.

She followed Nick out onto the porch. White clouds of icy snow swirled as a blue-and-white helicopter landed on the expanse of snow-covered lawn. The blades of the aircraft slowed. The door popped open and two people, a man and woman, both dressed in thick dark coats and winter boots, and wearing sunglasses, climbed out and strode through the snow toward the porch. As soon as the new arrivals were clear of the spinning blades, the helicopter took off with a roar, flying away over the mountain.

When the pair reached Kaitlyn and Nick, the man, tall with tousled sandy-blond hair, held out a piece of paper. The woman stood with her back to them, her gaze on the surrounding area, her right hand resting on the holstered weapon at her side. She was also tall, with dark hair pulled back into a straight ponytail. The collar of her coat was pulled up against the chill. There was something familiar about the way she carried herself that took Kaitlyn a moment to pinpoint. Then it registered. This female bodyguard had at one time been in law enforcement.

Nick compared the paper Collin had given him to the one he received from the bodyguard. "They match." He held out his hand. "Nick Delaney."

"Kyle Martin." The bodyguard grasped Nick's hand for a moment, then turned a charming smile toward Kaitlyn. "You must be the deputy."

Wariness flared inside her as she shook his hand. "Deputy Kaitlyn Lanz," she said. "How did you know who I was?"

"I bragged about you when I talked to them last night," Nick said. "I told them what a great job you've done protecting us. But it's time for you to get back to your job."

He wanted her gone? It was one thing for her to need to leave, to resume her duties, but another to realize he was ready for her to leave, as well. Hurt spread through her. She tamped it down.

"Shall we go inside?" The female bodyguard turned to face them.

"Yes, let's." Nick retreated indoors.

"After you, Deputy," Kyle said with another charming smile.

Kaitlyn entered the house with the two bodyguards close behind.

Kyle removed his sunglasses to reveal lively sky blue eyes. "Let me introduce my colleague, Simone Walker."

Simone peeled off her gloves; however, she didn't remove her sunglasses. "Mr. Delaney." After shaking Nick's hand, Simone held out her hand to Kaitlyn. "Deputy."

With a brisk shake, Kaitlyn said, "Nice to meet you, Ms. Walker."

"Call me Simone," she said. "Bring us up to speed on the situation."

For the next half hour, Nick and Kaitlyn tag teamed, telling the protection specialists the details of what had transpired over the past few days, showing them the security system and ending with the fact that, with their arrival, Kaitlyn needed to return to town and Nick would accompany her.

"You can rest assured, Deputy, we have things handled now," Kyle said.

Kaitlyn appreciated his confidence. She noted the wedding ring on his finger. Were he and Simone married? "That's good to hear."

"I'll walk the perimeter." Simone strode out the front door.

"So, what's it like to be a small-town sheriff's deputy?" Kyle asked, drawing her attention.

"I love it," she answered honestly. "I can't imagine living anywhere else. The people of Bristle Township are family. Serving the community is an honor." She saw the doubt in his eyes. "I take it you're not from a small town?"

"No. West Coast, born and raised on the beaches, relocated to Chicago via Boston. My wife is a surgeon at Heritage Hospital," he said.

"Oh. So you and Simone aren't a couple?" Nick asked.

Kaitlyn glanced at him. He'd had the same thought. It was strange how in sync they were at times.

Kyle laughed, clearly finding the idea amusing. "Hardly. But we work well together." He glanced at his watch. "I need to update our boss. Let him know we arrived." Kyle walked outside as he took his cell phone from his pocket.

Once she and Nick were alone, Kaitlyn said, "I should gather my things."

"I need to grab my wallet," Nick said. They ascended the stairs together. At the door to the room she'd stayed in, Nick said, "I'll meet you back downstairs in five?"

"Yes." Remembering the night they'd arrived, she quickly added, "And don't forget the flak vest."

"Right." He frowned. "Do I need to put it on?"

"It wouldn't hurt." And she'd put hers on, as well as being armed. Preparation could win the day.

With a nod, he strode down the hall. Kaitlyn watched him disappear into his room before she hurried to pack.

A strange mixture of relief and reluctance to be leaving the Delaney estate flooded her.

Nick could tell Kaitlyn was nervous on their drive down the mountain from the estate into town. She kept a vigilant eye on the road, her hands gripping the steering wheel with enough pressure to turn her knuckles white. The road conditions warranted caution, but he doubted it was the slickness of the fresh snow that had her so tense. As they passed the place in the road where Lexi's car had rammed into a tree, his heart thudded with grief beneath the heavy weight of the flak vest.

Learning of her death last night had been a blow he hadn't expected. He'd hoped she'd recover from being forced off the road. That she was gone made him even more determined to provide a safe life for Rosie.

Once the flash drive revealed its secrets, the threat to Rosie would be over and Nick would fight with everything he had for custody of the little girl. He understood why Kaitlyn insisted that Rosie's biological father be contacted. The man, whoever he was, had the right to know he had a child. But it was obvious to Nick that Lexi hadn't wanted the father to know about Rosie. There had to be a good reason.

When they reached town, Nick said, "You can drop me off at Fulman's Funeral Home. I'll come to the station as soon as I'm done."

Kaitlyn pulled into the parking lot of the funeral home. "Don't you want to know what's on the flash drive?"

"Of course I do," he said. "But I'm sure it will take Hannah some time to decrypt the drive. And I need to get this taken care of. For Lexi and Rosie."

Kaitlyn nodded with a tender gaze. "I'm sure Lexi would have appreciated how much you are doing for her and her child."

Sorrow welled in Nick's chest. "Thank you for that. I only wish she'd made it to me before the bad guys caught up to her."

"What happened to her is not your fault." Kaitlyn's tenderness turned fierce. "Don't you dare take that on."

He reached out to tuck a strand of her blond hair behind her ear. "You're right. I can only pray the men responsible will be brought to justice."

"One has already paid the ultimate price," she reminded him.

True—one of the two gunmen had been killed at the hospital. No doubt a hired thug. No, Nick wanted the person pulling the strings to pay.

Kaitlyn popped open her door.

"What are you doing?" he asked.

"Coming with you." She stepped out and shut the door.

He met her in front of the sheriff's department vehicle. "Why? You don't have to deal with this. It's more important you take the flash drive to Hannah."

"We will take it to her as soon as you're done here." She gestured toward the entrance.

Odd. He'd have thought she'd jump at the chance to be rid of him. He was pleased to have her support. Maybe revealing his sordid past last night had been a good thing if it softened her toward him.

A pickup truck sped into the parking lot, throwing snow and dirt into the air. Nick recognized the local mechanic's logo on the side of the door.

The truck skidded to a stop and the driver's-side door was flung open. Agent Jim Porter hopped out.

"Why's he driving Steve Grimes's truck?" Nick asked.

Kaitlyn made a low sound that resembled a growl. "Beats me."

"Where is it?" Porter demanded as he came to a stop in front of them.

"What?" Kaitlyn braced her feet apart and rested her hand on her holstered sidearm beneath the hem of her jacket.

"I just came from the sheriff's office," Porter said. "You found the flash drive. Hand it over."

Surprise flashed through Nick. The sheriff must have verified the agent really was who he claimed to be.

"We'll meet you at the sheriff's station," Kaitlyn said.

A dark blue utility vehicle pulled in behind the pickup and three men jumped out with guns. Kaitlyn shoved Nick behind her as she withdrew her sidearm. His heart jumped into his throat. He tugged her behind the front of her SUV where they would both be shielded.

Agent Porter spun around, drawing his weapon.

One of the men fired. The agent went down.

Nick reacted on instinct. He grabbed Porter's arm and dragged him through the dirty snow until he was safely hidden from the bad guys.

Kaitlyn shot back. Bullets riddled the vehicle.

"We're too exposed here," Kaitlyn muttered.

Nick glanced behind them. The entrance to the funeral home was fifty feet away. Could they make it?

TEN

Hunkered down behind the department-issued vehicle, Kaitlyn's gaze jumped between Nick and Agent Porter. Porter had been hit in the leg but was alive. And Nick had risked his own life to drag the Fed out of the line of fire and had taken off his jacket to press it against the other man's wound.

A stupid and heroic act that could have been costly. She praised God Nick hadn't been wounded, as well. At least he had on a flak vest, but still. Later she'd chew him out for his recklessness. For now, she needed to stay focused on keeping them all alive.

She, Nick and the Fed were pinned down. And she only had a few more rounds left in her weapon. There was no way they'd make the fifty feet to the entrance of the funeral home without being picked off like targets at a carnival shooting gallery.

The gunfire ceased and the silence made the hairs at the back of her neck quiver. Were the bad guys closing in?

"Deputy," a man's voice called out. "Give us the flash drive and we'll let you live."

"We don't have it," Nick shouted.

"Come on. Of course you do," the same man replied. "You wouldn't have left the safety of the estate if you didn't."

"No," Porter snapped. "You can't let them take it. If you do, Lexi will have died for nothing."

Nick grabbed the agent by the front of his shirt. "What did you get her into?"

"We don't have time for this," Kaitlyn said, despite how much she wanted to know the information.

She flattened herself on the ground so she could peer under the carriage of the vehicle. The men were using the pickup truck as cover. She could see three sets of feet. Scooting back, she held out her free hand to Porter. "Give me your gun."

Porter released the Glock to her. "Call for backup."

"On it." She grabbed her phone and dialed the station. When Carol, the dispatcher, answered, Kaitlyn explained the situation, then hung up. "We need to keep these guys at bay until help arrives." She sent up a quick prayer that God would send the cavalry before it was too late.

"What's it going to be, Deputy?" The man called out again. "Toss the flash drive our way and we'll leave."

With a gun in each hand, Kaitlyn positioned herself so that if anyone rounded the corner of the vehicle on either side of them, she had a clear shot. "Why should we believe you?"

"You really don't have a choice," he called back, definitely closer now.

A strange calmness descended over Kaitlyn. Part of the job was being prepared to take a life and give her life. She regretted that Nick was here and would also suffer her fate. She could take out two of the assailants, but she wasn't sure she'd be able to get all three before one of them fired back.

The wail of a siren rent the air. There was shouting and then the roar of an engine as the assailants scurried back into their vehicle and drove away.

Cautiously, Kaitlyn peered around the edge of the front end of her vehicle in time to see the assailants escape. Relief washed over her, making her limbs shake. She holstered her sidearm and tucked Agent Porter's weapon beneath her belt at her waist next to her holster.

Alex's SUV skidded to a halt, sliding slightly in the slick snow. He jumped out. "Kaitlyn!"

She stood, her legs rubbery, but she remained upright. "Here. We have a man down."

Alex rushed forward. "We received numerous calls of shots fired. An ambulance is on the way. What happened?"

"We were ambushed," she said. "Three men. Dark blue utility vehicle. They wanted the flash drive."

Nick, still crouched beside Porter, said to the downed agent, "Tell us now. What is this all about?"

Porter trained his gaze on the sheriff. "Holtsen Pharmaceuticals has been selling tainted drugs and suppressing adverse side effects that have left many dead or comatose."

"How was Lexi involved?" Nick asked.

Porter flicked his gaze to Nick. "She had been living with the CEO, Harrison Reece. She gathered intel that proved Harrison and the company knowingly kept the drugs on the market despite the internal reports from their scientist saying the drugs were contaminated."

"And they killed her for it," Nick said. "We have to make this man pay."

"I've been in contact with the special agent in charge at the DC office," Alex said. "He told me the same thing, which is why I told Agent Porter you had the flash drive."

"You need to get the evidence to DC," Porter insisted. "It's the only way to stop Harrison Reece and Holtsen Pharmaceuticals before anyone else dies."

"I'll take it," Nick said. "I won't let Lexi's death be in vain."

Incredulous, Kaitlyn stared. "How do you intend to transport the flash drive without your armored Humvee? Those men aren't going to stop."

Nick's dark eyes flashed with determination. "I'll fly it there."

"Again, driving from here to Denver to catch a flight—"

He held up a hand, cutting her off. "Not Denver. We keep a hangar on the mountain."

There was an airstrip at the top of Eagle Peak near the Eagle Peak Resort. "Your family has a plane there?"

"We keep two there, actually. Ian and Dad prefer the Learjet. We can take the Cirrus." He took out his phone. "I'll have the plane readied."

"I'll drive you up the mountain," Alex said.

Mind reeling, Kaitlyn said, "You're a civilian. I'll go."

Nick smiled. "I was hoping you'd say that."

Tamping down her frustration, she clarified, "You'll stay, and I'll go."

He shook his head. "My plane. I'm going."

Stubborn man. Didn't Nick realize how dangerous this would be? Kaitlyn fisted her hands in frustration. She turned to Alex for support, but he had already moved away to greet the paramedics and direct them to Porter.

If Alex wouldn't back her on this, then the only thing

she could do was stick close to Nick and make sure he didn't get himself killed trying to avenge his friend's death. For Rosie's sake, she told herself. Okay, she'd admit her feelings had changed after learning more about him while at the estate, seeing him with Rosie and now his actions here with Porter. But that didn't mean she was developing feelings for Nick.

Once Porter was in the ambulance and on his way to the hospital, Alex said, "You two ride with me. I'll have someone come back for your vehicle."

As Alex drove toward town, he said, "You both are in need of some supplies. We'll stop at the station before heading up the mountain."

Because Main Street was cordoned off for the Christmas craft fair, Alex took the residential route to the back alley behind the department building. He backed his vehicle into a spot near the door. Kaitlyn glanced around, noting the multitude of cars parked along the side streets. Music and laughter drifted on the air from the holiday festival, which was in full swing on Main Street.

Nick stopped next to her. "What's going on in town?"

"The annual Christmas bazaar," she said. "All the local craftspeople set up booths along the sidewalk, and the stores have specials to draw in the tourists either coming from or going up the mountain."

"Sounds fun. I've only been to the open marketplaces in Europe," he said.

"I'm sure our humble craft fair won't compare," she said. Their lives were so different. She'd never been beyond the Rockies and had only seen the Pacific Ocean once, when she was young. While he'd traveled the world.

Another reason for her to keep her heart from becoming attached to Nick. She could never be enough for such a globe-trotting man.

Nick followed Alex into the sheriff's station. Kaitlyn hesitated as a chill swept over her. The uncanny sensation of being watched made the skin on her arms prickle with foreboding. She glanced around, searching for the source of her unease, but there was no one in sight.

She hurried inside the station but couldn't shake the dread clawing through her. It was only a matter of time before Reece's men attacked again.

Nick stood off to the side of the small tactical room inside the sheriff's department building, unsure what he could do to help as Alex grabbed a duffel bag and proceeded to fill it with extra ammo and radios.

"You remember how to use these, right?" Alex asked, indicating the Taser he now held.

Not long ago, Alex had given Nick and Brady a lesson on Tasers. "Yes, I remember how the Taser works."

"What does that mean?" Kaitlyn asked as she joined them.

Nick exchanged a glance with Alex. "Oh, you know. There's nothing like experience."

She narrowed her gaze. Nick could see the questions forming in her eyes. He wasn't sure he wanted to admit he'd voluntarily allowed Alex to tase him. It was an experience Nick didn't relish repeating, but it was good to know what would happen. The only way Nick could describe it was that it was like having a full-body muscle cramp that lasted until the electric current was cut off. Three seconds in Nick's case, but it had seemed like a lifetime.

Alex spoke, drawing their attention. "You don't know

what you will encounter when you get to Washington, DC. I will let the special agent in charge there know to expect you and have his agents waiting for your arrival. But according to Agent Porter, Reece has wealthy friends in high places. Porter isn't sure who to trust besides his SAC. That's one of the reasons Porter is on his own here."

"He went rogue," Nick said. "I knew there was something fishy about him."

"Going rogue isn't cool," Alex agreed. "But he can't prove his case without the information that Lexi obtained."

"Surely the victims of this drug have filed lawsuits?" Kaitlyn asked.

"According to Special Agent in Charge Jeff Lester, Holtsen Pharmaceuticals has paid off every lawsuit lodged against them," Alex replied. "They have deep pockets and can afford it."

"Then it's that much more important we get the flash drive into the right hands," Nick said.

"Shouldn't we let Hannah try to decrypt the flash drive first?" Kaitlyn asked.

"We can have her try or at least make a copy. She just returned from the accident scene," Alex said. "Kaitlyn, take it down to her. Nick, a word."

Kaitlyn hesitated, then gave a sharp nod and left Nick and Alex alone.

"What's up?" Nick asked as soon as Kaitlyn was out of the room.

"I wanted you to know I located Lexi's family," he said.

Nick's heart rate sped up. "And? Did you tell them

about Rosie?" Would Lexi's family want custody of the baby?

"Her parents are deceased. I managed to talk to a cousin in Singapore who says she hadn't seen Lexi in a decade. I got the impression she wasn't too broken up to hear of her death. I mentioned Rosie, but she cut me off. Apparently, the Eng family disowned Lexi when she refused to return home after college."

"That's sad." Nick understood what it was like to not have one's family's approval, but he'd never considered what it would be like to be completely cut out of their lives. That must have hurt Lexi. She'd never mentioned the rift with her parents when Nick had known her. The desire to call his brother and father to assure himself all was well was strong but would have to wait.

He ached for Lexi not having a relationship with her family. However, that was one less obstacle to Nick gaining custody of Rosie. He was thankful he wasn't navigating through this situation alone. He had his friendship with Alex.

And Kaitlyn. Though he wasn't exactly sure how to categorize their relationship. If he were honest with himself, he'd admit he cared for the woman in ways he'd never allowed himself to care about anyone else before.

And that was almost as scary as being ambushed by armed men.

Curiosity burning as to why Alex needed to talk to Nick, Kaitlyn slowed her steps as she went down the stairs to the lower part of the building where the forensic lab was located. Finding out what the two men were discussing would have to wait. She absurdly wondered if it had to do with her. Would Nick ask Alex about her past?

She wasn't even sure if Alex was privy to that information. Sheriff Ryder had been, but only because she'd told him. What if Nick mentioned that she'd practically run from him when he'd pressed her for answers? Would Alex then go snooping into her past?

Stop it! She wasn't normally one to be paranoid. Especially not over being excluded from a conversation.

She knocked on the doorjamb outside the lab.

Hannah waved Kaitlyn into her sanctuary. "What's going on? Your brow's all furrowed."

Purposely clearing her expression, Kaitlyn pulled the flash drive from her pocket. She didn't need to let on to Hannah her confusing feelings for Nick. "There's an encrypted file on this. Is there any way you could try to decrypt it for me quickly? Or at the very least make a copy?"

"I can certainly try," Hannah said, taking the USB stick and plugging it into her state-of-the-art computer equipment.

The same window popped up that had appeared on Nick's computer. Kaitlyn gave Hannah the password, Rosie's birth date.

"This is an encryption I've never seen," Hannah said. "I can make a copy to work on, but I don't know that I can decrypt the file within a reasonable amount of time. It might take me a month or two."

"We don't even have two minutes," Kaitlyn said. "Make a copy and do what you can. I need to take the original with me."

Hannah's fingers flew over the keyboard. "Where you going?"

"Washington, DC."

With a concerned glance, Hannah asked, "Alone?"

Kaitlyn shook her head. "No. Nick Delaney's coming with me."

A smile spread across her friend's face. "You and Nick have been spending a lot of time together. Maya, Leslie and I were just talking yesterday about the fact that you are staying out at the Delaney estate." Hannah removed the flash drive from her computer and handed it to Kaitlyn. "What's it like out there? I've never been."

Uncomfortable with the fact that her friends were talking about her, Kaitlyn tucked the flash drive into the pocket of her coat. She couldn't blame them. She was sure the whole town was in a twitter over the fact that she was staying at the Delaney mansion. Despite the fact she was protecting Rosie, under orders from her boss, she had no doubts tongues were wagging. However, she couldn't do anything about the gossip.

She sighed. "It's actually very nice. It's been an interesting visit. I've learned a lot about the Delaneys."

Speculation gleamed in Hannah's green eyes. "About Nick specifically? Do tell."

Heat flushed through Kaitlyn's cheeks and down her neck. She cleared her throat. "It's not like that. I was more concerned with keeping everyone safe. The bad guys attempted to breach twice and almost succeeded once."

"I heard about that," Hannah said. "But you fended them off. Good for you."

"I did what I was trained to do," Kaitlyn replied. It always amazed her when people were surprised by her ability to do her job. "Plus, the Fed showed up." She wasn't above giving credit where credit was due. "He was wounded and is now at the hospital. So it's up to Nick and me to transport the flash drive to DC."

"Where's the baby?" Hannah's smile was tender. "I hear she's adorable."

Kaitlyn agreed. Little Rosie was so cute. Affection for the baby flooded her veins. It would be hard when the time came that Kaitlyn wouldn't be a part of the child's life. "At the estate. Nick hired professional bodyguards to protect her while we are away."

Wagging her eyebrows, Hannah commented, "Gotta love a guy who's willing to go the extra mile for a tiny infant."

Kaitlyn's heart fluttered. "Yeah, something like that."

Love? The word stuck in her chest like a thorn. She didn't love Nick. Couldn't love him. That would be beyond ridiculous. Yet the urge to rub at the aching spot beneath her breastbone was strong. Forcing herself to ignore the sensation and the silly sentiment, she said, "Thank you for your help. I'll talk to you later."

Kaitlyn hurried back upstairs and found Nick waiting with the sheriff's jacket on.

He must have seen the question on her face because he shrugged and said, "My jacket was ruined."

Right. When he'd used it to stem the blood flow from Porter's leg wound. "You did a really reckless thing back at the funeral home."

His eyebrows rose. "I did?"

Frustration burned in her gut. Of course, he would be flippant about the situation. "You risked your life by pulling Porter to safety."

His expression was mockingly innocent. "I shouldn't have?"

"Yes. I mean, no." He so easily flustered her. How did she get it through his head not to put his life in danger? "I mean, you're a civilian. I should have done it."

"You were shooting back at the bad guys at the time," he pointed out. "You're not a superhero who can perform two death-defying feats at once."

She rolled her eyes and shook her head. "Don't use logic on me."

He laughed, and she smiled, feeling some of the tension in her shoulders ease. "Thank you for not getting yourself killed."

"I aim to please," he quipped.

Alex walked out of his office. "Here's the plan. Daniel and Chase are both going to park their vehicles beside my car. We're going to play a little shell game. I'll take the lead and head to the Delaney estate. You two will hide in Daniel's vehicle and he'll drive toward Eagle Peak Resort via the backside mountain pass. And Chase will take the highway for Denver. Hopefully, Reece's men won't know which of the vehicles you two are in."

"Won't they see us walk out the door and get into one of them?" Nick asked.

"We have that covered, as well. All the doors will be open. You two will get into my vehicle, hunker down, then climb out and get into Daniel's. You'll need to stay down and out of sight. It will be tight, but you can do it."

Grateful for her new boss's quick and strategic thinking, Kaitlyn said, "Sounds like a solid idea."

Within a few minutes, Daniel and Chase both arrived and came inside the station. After both were brought up to speed on the situation, the five of them left the building with Nick in the middle. Kaitlyn hoped that, with Nick wearing the sheriff's jacket, sunglasses and a department-issued hat, anyone watching wouldn't pick him out of the group.

Kaitlyn and Nick climbed into the back of Alex's vehicle. Daniel and Chase had backed up alongside. Kaitlyn and Nick crouched down and crawled from Alex's car to Daniel's. Both deputies and the sheriff closed the doors simultaneously before climbing behind their respective wheels and starting their engines.

Over the radio, Alex said, "Take off."

Daniel drove through the back alleys of town to avoid the festive crowds. Kaitlyn shifted on the floorboards, trying to get comfortable for the drive up the mountain. Nick had his back leaned against the door and his legs drawn up so that he could rest his arms on his legs.

"You're like Gumby," she muttered.

"It pays to stay limber," he said. "When we return to the estate, we can work out the kinks in the dojo."

Remembering the last time they'd sparred sent a flush creeping up her neck. She'd been surprised by his prowess. But then, learning he'd been trained at a young age in martial arts explained his abilities. She didn't comment because once this task of delivering the flash drive to the FBI was done, there would be no reason for her to return to the estate.

Daniel beeped his horn. "I feel like a salmon swimming upstream in the Snake River. I thought there'd be less traffic taking the alleys, but apparently so did everyone else."

"Keep an eye out for anybody following us," Kaitlyn said.

"Roger that," Daniel replied. "So far, so good."

"Alex found Lexi's family," Nick said softly.

"Really?" Kaitlyn studied him. The sadness in his eyes tangled up her insides. "And?"

"Her family had disowned her. They don't want Rosie."

A spark of anger ignited in her. How could they not want Rosie? "Their loss."

"Okay, we're leaving town proper," Daniel said. "But I think we've picked up a tail. A small white pickup truck. I've seen it around town the last few days but haven't gotten a good look at the driver."

Kaitlyn fisted her hands against the urge to see for herself. "I guess our shell game didn't work."

Nick scoffed. "This Holtsen company has money to burn. There's probably a whole slew of Reece's henchmen in town. There could be someone following each vehicle."

"Should we abort?" Daniel asked.

Nick shook his head. "We can't. We have to figure out a way to get up the mountain."

There was more than one way up the mountain. Though Kaitlyn knew Nick wasn't going to like what she had in mind, she said, "I have an idea. Just keep driving toward the mountain pass. I'll make a call."

ELEVEN

Huddled on the floorboards in the back seat of Daniel's patrol car, Nick listened to Kaitlyn explain what she needed from her friend Leslie Quinn with a mix of stunned horror and anxiety tightening his chest.

The second she hung up, he said, "Horses? You've got to be joking."

"No, I'm not." She tucked her phone into the pocket of the jacket, then rifled through the duffel bag she'd set on the back seat. She stuffed her pockets with extra ammo clips.

"You know I don't ride." Was she purposely messing with him?

"Trust me," she said, her gaze earnest and so pretty as she handed him a Taser. "I've been teaching people to ride my whole life. I'm not going to let anything bad happen to you."

His mouth dried. The metal of the Taser was cold against his palm. The problem was that he did trust her. But a horse? The thought sent a shudder through him.

"It's going to be okay, Nick," she said.

Apparently, his expression had given him away. "I

know. I just have to wrap my head around the situation. I had a bad experience with horses when I was young."

"What happened?"

"One of the boarding schools I attended had an equestrian program and they insisted that we learn to ride." He couldn't keep the derision from his tone. "On the very first lesson, the horse they put me on spooked, and next thing I knew, I was flat on my back with the horse standing over me. I couldn't breathe. I couldn't move. I thought for sure I was a goner."

Empathy softened her gaze. "How old were you?"

"Nine. An incident like that leaves a mark."

"I can imagine how scary that must have been." She touched his hand. "Remember what you told me last night? *With God, we don't have to be imprisoned by fear.*"

In theory that sounded doable. He'd been working on facing his emotional fears. Would facing his fears be so doable in reality when he was atop a twelve-hundred-pound horse again? Would God protect him from falling?

Nick's gaze drank in Kaitlyn's beautiful face. Admiration for her dedication to her job and her community wound through him. He was in danger of falling in so many different ways that falling off a horse was the least of his worries. He was going to need all the help God would grace him with to not fall in love with Kaitlyn.

He jerked his gaze from her and tucked the Taser into the inside pocket of the jacket he wore.

"We still have a tail," Daniel said. "We left town, so there's no mistaking that the truck is following us."

"When you get to mile marker eighteen, pull off the road. If the truck goes past, great. If the truck stops, too, then you'll need to keep the driver occupied while we climb out and disappear into the woods."

"Got it," Daniel said.

"We'll meet Leslie on the upper mountain trail," she said. "Then ride the rest of the way to Eagle Peak Resort."

"The Cirrus will be gassed and ready to go." Nick would just have to figure out how to sit a horse without toppling over.

"Just about there," Daniel said. "Bail out on the right side of the vehicle."

"Perfect," Kaitlyn said. To Nick, she said, "Be ready."

Tension revved through Nick's body. Be ready? To escape into the woods, ride a horse and fly off to DC with evidence of a bad man's dealings. Why should he be anxious? Just another adventure. Right? He blew out a breath.

He might never have done any of these things before, but he was prepared to do whatever it took to bring these people to justice so that Lexi hadn't died in vain and to keep Rosie safe.

The car slowed, then pulled off the paved road onto the uneven dirt shoulder and came to a stop. Daniel cut the engine.

"Our shadow stopped about twenty feet back," Daniel told them.

"Can you distract him?" Kaitlyn asked.

"Of course," he replied.

"Be careful, Daniel," she said. "We can't lose you."

Nick peered at Kaitlyn as a thread of jealousy wound through him. Did Kaitlyn have a thing for her coworker?

Daniel barked out a laugh. "I'm not worried. You two be safe. And tell Leslie to check in." Daniel opened the driver's-side door and stepped out. As he passed by the left rear passenger window, Nick saw that he had his weapon drawn and ready.

"Out of the vehicle," Daniel yelled. Then he moved out of view.

Kaitlyn's hand on Nick's knee startled him. His gaze met hers.

"Pop open the door just enough to ease out. Then hustle into the bushes," she said.

He gave her a nod, then maneuvered himself around into a position that would let him open the door. A blast of cold winter air hit him in the face, sending a shiver down his spine.

Stepping out took a little exertion, which helped to chase away the chill. He bumped his knee on the seat and hit his funny bone on the edge of the door. He gritted his teeth against the shooting pain. He was glad to see that Daniel had parked the vehicle at an angle. There was no way the guy in the truck would be able to see them.

Nick made it out of the vehicle. His feet squished into the snow piled along the edge of the shoulder. Cold seeped through his loafers as he hurried to the cover of snow-dusted bushes, the branches scratching at his clothes. Kaitlyn quickly followed.

"Shouldn't we make sure Daniel's okay?" Nick asked her.

The look of approval she sent his way warmed him inside. "Yes. You stay here. I'll take a look."

Before he could protest at being sidelined, she moved away. After a moment, she returned and settled back next to Nick in a crouch. "The guy in the white truck took off. Daniel is getting back in his car. He'll head to town."

"Good," Nick said. "You were really worried about him."

She slanted him a glance. "Of course."

"Are you and he…?" Nick resisted the urge to tug at the collar of his sweater beneath the sheriff's jacket.

"What? Why would you even ask that?" She shook her head. "No. He's my colleague and my friend."

Relieved and also a bit flummoxed that he'd even thought to ask the question, he shrugged. "Just checking."

She made a scoffing noise and rose to her feet. "Let's go." She marched forward, seemingly oblivious to the thick underbrush scraping at her pants legs.

Nick looked down at the loafers he wore. Great. He'd expected to go from the car to the plane to another car then to a warm and dry building. Not traipsing through the wilderness. He carefully picked a path forward behind her. "I should've worn my new hiking boots I bought that I've never tried."

Kaitlyn called over her shoulder, "You'd only get blisters if you'd done that."

"I'll probably still get blisters. These aren't the best shoes to be tramping around in the woods."

After what seemed like hours with the cold seeping through his clothes to prickle his skin, but was closer to fifteen minutes, they came out of the trees onto a wide dirt- and snow-covered path leading up the mountain. Kaitlyn's friend Leslie, wearing athletic clothes, her dark blond hair pulled back into a high ponytail and earbuds hanging around her neck, stood there holding the reins of two saddled horses.

As soon as Leslie saw them, she dropped the reins and hurried to greet them. Amazingly, both horses stood still, not moving a muscle. Nick eyed the two big, beautiful animals, one brown and one yellow. Both looked strong and fast and had saddles really high off the ground. His stomach churned.

Normally, he didn't have an issue with heights. He'd dived off cliffs and out of airplanes, rock climbed on some of the country's most famous mountains. But the thought of climbing onto a horse's back again filled him with dread.

"Leslie, this is Nick Delaney," Kaitlyn said. "Nick, Leslie."

Nick shook the woman's hand. "Nice to formally meet you. Aren't you freezing?"

"Likewise. And no. My running gear is made for this weather." Curiosity burned in Leslie's gaze. "What's going on?"

Kaitlyn succinctly explained the situation. "There's a plane waiting for us at the top of the mountain."

"I could come with you," Leslie offered.

"I appreciate the offer, but we've got this," Kaitlyn said. "Right, Nick?"

Nick tore his gaze away from the horses. "Right. We've got this." Even to his own ears he didn't sound convincing.

Leslie studied him for a moment before turning her gaze on Kaitlyn. "Now I understand why you asked for Groot and Star Lord. They are both sure-footed. Groot would be better for a novice."

"Thank you, Leslie," Kaitlyn said.

"I take it you're a fan of science fiction movies," Nick said, his gaze back on the two animals patiently waiting. "Which one is Groot?"

"The brown one with the black mane."

He swallowed. Groot looked anything but tame or docile. The horse's muscles were lean and sleek. His dark eyes seemed to bore into Nick. Did the horse understand the word *novice*?

Turning to Leslie, he asked, "How are you going to get back home?"

She looked at him funny. "I'm on a run." She picked up the earbuds and put them in her ears. "Nothing unusual to see here."

Gesturing to the horses, Nick asked, "How did you get them here?"

"We came through the woods from my place," Leslie answered.

"Daniel wants you to check in," Kaitlyn said.

Leslie made a face. "I'll touch base with Alex." She took off at a run back down the hiking trail.

After Leslie disappeared around a curve in the trail, Nick turned to Kaitlyn. "She doesn't like Daniel?"

"Grade-school rivals. Come on. Let's get you on Groot." Kaitlyn walked over to the horses. She checked the saddles on both horses by flipping one stirrup over the saddle and then adjusted the leather strap under each beast's belly.

He stopped a safe distance in front of Groot and stared into his eyes. "You and me, we're going to be okay, right?" he asked the horse. "Man to man. You're not going to throw me or anything, are you?"

Kaitlyn chuckled softly. "You do know he's not going to answer you."

"It doesn't hurt to set boundaries," Nick said.

Smiling, Kaitlyn said, "Hold out your arm, palm down, and wait for him to sniff."

"Like you do when you greet a new dog?"

"Exactly. The horsemen's handshake. It's a way for

him to give you permission to ride him. Like this." She demonstrated with Star Lord, stretching her arm forward with the back of her hand toward the horse's nose. After a heartbeat, Star Lord snuffled the back of her hand, then blew out a noisy breath. Kaitlyn rubbed his forehead and stroked a hand down his neck. "Hi, there."

Tentatively, Nick held out his arm, giving Groot access to sniff the back of his hand. The horse's dark eyes never left Nick's face. Groot stretched out his neck to take a quick sniff of Nick. Then he lifted his nose and gave a shake of his head, his bridle jangling.

"Did he just say no?" Nervous energy raced along Nick's limbs.

"Give it another try," she said. "And move closer."

Stilling the anxious storm inside his gut, Nick stepped closer and held out the back of his hand. After a few seconds, Groot sniffed his hand, then gave it a nudge.

"Okay, he's willing," Kaitlyn said. "Slowly move to his left side and gently stroke your hand down the side of his neck."

With his heart beating in his ears, Nick did as she'd instructed. The horse's coat was warm and silky beneath Nick's palm.

"Good job. Now watch me. I'm going to demonstrate how you'll mount the horse, but don't do anything until I'm there to help you." She took Star Lord's reins in her hand, then moved to his left side. Lifting her left foot, she placed it in the stirrup. Then she fisted a handful of the horse's mane with one hand, grabbed the horn on the saddle and pulled herself up, swinging her right leg over the horse's behind before sitting in the saddle. "See? Simple."

Nick marveled. Maybe simple for her.

She did the action in reverse, looking so graceful and natural. Sweat broke out along Nick's back. He dried his damp palms on the front of his slacks.

Letting Star Lord's reins drop to the ground again, she picked up Groot's reins, lifted them over his head and came to stand next to Nick. She grasped the horn of the saddle and rocked the saddle. The horse shifted its feet. "Good boy." She patted his shoulder.

"What did you just do?"

"His stance was uneven," she said. "It will be easier on both of you now that he's standing square."

Nick had no idea what she was talking about but decided he didn't need to know.

Kaitlyn tugged at Nick's elbow, positioning him so that he was next to the middle of the horse facing the horse's head. "You don't want to stand by his shoulder when you're mounting. If he spooks, he could send you flying."

"Good to know." There was so much more to this horse business than he'd have thought. He'd refused to return to the riding lessons after the incident. He hadn't gone near a horse since and had put the whole thing out of his mind until Kaitlyn came into his life.

"Hand position when mounting is important," Kaitlyn said. "With your left hand you'll take the reins and a chunk of mane." She demonstrated.

Groot's head came up.

"This lets the horse know you're preparing to sit in the saddle," she continued. She released her hold on the horse's mane and moved aside while handing Nick the reins.

He took the leather straps in his left hand and reached up to capture a handful of the dark mane with the same hand. "Are you sure this won't hurt him? I mean, I'll be pulling his hair."

"Horses have a whole different set of nerve endings in their manes and tails. Nothing like humans. You won't hurt him."

"If you say so," he muttered. "Now what?"

"With your right hand grab the horn," she said.

He reached up for the hooked piece at the front of the saddle.

Kaitlyn moved to Groot's head. "I'll hold him to be safe. Now, lift your left foot into the stirrup but only put the ball of your foot in."

"Whew. You're tall, Groot," Nick muttered.

"Do you need a boost?" she asked.

Not for the life of him would he want her help. He was a man, after all. He could do this. Thankfully he was limber enough to get his foot up into the stirrup. "It's in."

"Push up to a standing position, swing your right leg over the back end and then gently sit. Once you're in position I can help you find the other stirrup."

"Here we go, boy," Nick murmured. He pulled himself so he was standing on his left leg in the stirrup. Then he awkwardly lifted his leg up and over the saddle. He tried to ease into a sitting position, but it was more of a plop.

"Ouch." He gritted his teeth.

"I said gently."

His nostrils flared. "Yes, you did."

He rooted around with his right foot for the stirrup but the thing was being elusive. Then she was there helping him, her hand on his calf, guiding his foot onto the tread. She adjusted the length of the stirrups, making him more comfortable. "Thank you."

Staring down at her, he liked the way the winter sun

streaming through the canopy of tree branches shone on her honey-blond hair.

The horse pawed at the ground.

Nick patted his neck.

Kaitlyn swung up on Star Lord, who didn't move a muscle as she settled into the saddle.

"Why did I get the horse that's restless?" he asked.

She glanced at him with a rare grin that set his heart to pounding. "You didn't. But you're a novice and he knows it."

"How can he tell?"

"Horses are smarter than you think. They can tell when somebody who's never been on a horse is sitting on them. It makes them jittery."

"Great." His hand tightened around the horn.

"Keep the reins loose and hold them in your left hand," she said. "Let's ride."

She made a clicking sound into her cheek and Star Lord moved up the trail.

Nick tried clucking into his cheek, but Groot didn't budge. "Kait, help?"

Twisting in her seat, she said, "Don't worry. Groot will follow us."

After a tense, still moment, Groot huffed out a breath, then walked forward. Nick nearly lost his balance. He leaned over the horn and hung on, but gradually he relaxed and sat upright. His family was never going to believe this. He didn't believe it. If anyone other than Kaitlyn had suggested they ride up the mountain trail, he'd have refused. But he doubted he could refuse Kaitlyn anything.

A fate nearly as terrifying as falling off Groot.

* * *

Twenty minutes later, Kaitlyn brought Star Lord to a halt to allow Nick and Groot to catch up. She had to admit he was doing well after such a terrifying experience when he was young. Of course, Groot was a well-trained quarter horse, accustomed to inexperienced riders. Because Leslie was part of the county's mounted patrol, she was often called upon to bring Groot when they had a lost soul to find. More often than not, a lost hiker had never ridden a horse, and Groot was very tolerant.

"I'm going to need a spinal adjustment when this is over," Nick said as Groot drew abreast of Star Lord. "I feel every bump and root and rock in the trail."

Kaitlyn studied his posture. "Don't hold yourself so stiff. Let your body relax into the motion of the horse."

"That's easy for you to say."

"Don't worry, Nick. It's not too much farther." She urged Star Lord to pick up the pace.

When they hit the edge of the forest, Kaitlyn reined Star Lord to a stop. Groot halted, as well.

"We'll ride along the edge of the tree line," she told Nick as she scanned the cleared airstrip ahead of them. "Less visible that way, in case Reece has men stationed here."

Nick nodded in agreement, still looking very much out of his element of sports cars and black-tie parties. But he was trying, and Kaitlyn couldn't deny the admiration swelling within her.

When they made it behind the hangar, Kaitlyn hopped off her horse and dropped the reins. She called the resort and asked for someone to come take the horses to the hotel's stables. Leslie would retrieve them later.

"You make it look so easy. Kait, I'll need assistance."

Smiling inwardly because she was sure it cost him to ask for help, Kaitlyn proceeded to talk him through the dismount. When his feet landed on the ground, he stumbled backward. She reflexively grabbed his shoulders in a steadying grip.

He turned to face her. He was inches away. Their gazes locked.

"You did well," she said. Why was she so breathless?

"Thanks to you," he replied.

His gaze dropped to her lips and then returned to her eyes. Attraction flared. He reached up to tuck a stray strand of her hair behind her ear, his fingers lingering, his touch electrifying. Slowly, he traced the line of her jaw with a featherlight touch. "Kaitlyn."

A shiver of yearning coursed through her veins. But now was not the time. They had an important mission to accomplish. Giving in to this thing arcing between them wouldn't be smart. She cleared her throat and stepped back. "We need to get going."

Dropping his hand to his side, he nodded. Resignation flashed in his eyes. She hesitated with regret for letting the moment pass by, but it couldn't be helped. She needed to stay focused.

Inside the steel-beamed, metal, sixty-foot-high hangar, Nick led the way to the office. The woman behind the counter smiled brightly. "Mr. Delaney. The plane's ready to go."

He wrote out their destination and flight plan on the log sheet. Once the paperwork was completed, Nick and Kaitlyn hurried over to his plane, a beautiful, sleek aircraft with red stripes that made her think of a race car. A single jet engine rode on the top of the plane in front of the V-shaped tail. Figured Nick would have a top-of-the-line, sporty aircraft.

The door was open, and the folding steps extended out.

"This is sweet," Kaitlyn said, impressed and a bit awed.

Nick smoothed a hand over the polished white wing. "A Cirrus jet with a few custom modifications, including high-tech autopiloting and safety features. The best money can buy."

"Of course," she said, unable to keep the dry tone out of her voice.

With a shrug, he said, "What can I say? Wealth comes with privilege."

"And responsibility," she added. "The amount of money you spent on this could help a lot of people."

One eyebrow arched. "You think we only spend our wealth on ourselves?" He shook his head, his expression darkening with clear disappointment. He held out his hand. "Ladies first."

Hesitating, she had to admit she had no idea if the Delaneys were charitable or not. A prick of guilt stung her, making her amend that thought. The Delaney family had rebuilt the sheriff's department after a fire destroyed most of the building, and they gave to the church, if the church secretary was to be believed. And Kaitlyn couldn't think of a reason Joann would make up a story. And Maya had said that the Delaneys had covered Brady's summer camp expense last year.

Kaitlyn had always assumed it was Ian behind the giving. But was Nick as generous?

Something she definitely needed to discover before she made any more snap judgments about him.

Aware that he waited to help her onto the plane, she grasped his hand, their palms fitting together nicely. Warmth shimmied through her and she was afraid her cheeks were turning pink. She stepped up the stairs and paused to glance back at him. He let go of her and tucked his hands into his jacket pockets.

Missing his touch, she sighed at her own confusing emotions, boarded the plane and came to an abrupt halt as her gaze landed on a man in a wool coat with graying hair.

In his hand he held a Glock, aimed at her chest.

TWELVE

"Come in, Mr. Delaney," a man called out from within the plane. "Join us, please."

Adrenaline spiking at the unfamiliar voice, Nick halted on the stairs to the plane's small cabin. Kaitlyn blocked his path. She'd stopped in the doorway and had drawn her weapon. His heart stalled.

Kaitlyn glanced over her shoulder at Nick. He sucked in a sharp breath at the distress on her lovely face. She ducked her head and moved farther into the plane, allowing Nick to enter. The interior of the custom-built personal jet consisted of two pairs of single bucket seats facing each other, with a small table between them, on either side of a short aisle. Headroom was limited, but there was ample space to maneuver within.

Nick's gaze locked onto an older man who sat in one of the forward-facing plush leather seats. He had salt-and-pepper hair and wore a cashmere coat over a very expensive-looking Italian suit. And held a gun in his hand aimed at Kaitlyn's heart.

Another man sat in the copilot's seat. He was one of the thugs who'd attacked them in the hospital and who'd tried to breach the estate. He also held a weapon trained on Kaitlyn.

"Put the gun on the floor, Deputy," the well-dressed man instructed.

"No." Kaitlyn held steady. "You put down yours."

The man shook his head with a twist of his lips. "Really, Deputy, you should do as I ask."

In a swift move, the thug seated in the copilot's seat vaulted to his feet and rammed his shoulder into Nick's gut. Momentarily stunned, Nick doubled over, his eyes watering.

Kaitlyn swiveled toward Nick. The thug then rushed her, his big, beefy hands wrenching the gun from her grip.

The weapon skittered across the floor beneath the seats.

"Both of you take a seat," the well-dressed man demanded.

The thug pushed Kaitlyn into the seat across from the man in charge. Her expression was filled with anger.

Nick figured she was mad at herself for letting the big guy get the better of her. Nick understood her frustration. The guy had moved so quickly, Nick hadn't been prepared. He would be if there was a next time. He took the unoccupied forward-facing seat across from their captor. His mind whirled. Could he reach underneath the seat for Kaitlyn's weapon? Was there something else he could use as a defense against these men?

"I take it you're Harrison Reece," Kaitlyn said, her voice rife with disdain.

The man's mouth curved in a semblance of a smile, but his cold blue eyes were empty of emotion. "What gave me away?"

"Your arrogance," Kaitlyn shot back.

"Nice comeback, Deputy. Hand over your cell phones."

The thug moved from the cockpit to take their reluctantly produced phones. He dropped them into a black bag he stashed under the copilot's seat before sitting back down.

Harrison turned his gaze to Nick. "I knew it would be only a matter of time before you showed up here." He flicked a glance at Kaitlyn. "Nice strategy, trying to confuse my men by having the other deputies going in different directions, hoping my men wouldn't know whom to follow."

Nick met Kaitlyn's gaze and saw his own frustration reflected in her eyes.

"What did you do with the pilot?" Kaitlyn asked.

Harrison kept his gaze on Nick. "Mr. Delaney is the pilot."

Nick held the man's gaze, but he could feel Kaitlyn staring at him. He may have forgotten to mention that he was planning on flying the jet. "And what if I refuse?"

Harrison's malicious expression sent a chill down Nick's spine. "I'm sure we can think of all kinds of things to do with Deputy Lanz that would give you incentive to cooperate."

Nick growled. "You touch a hair on her head and you're a dead man."

The thought of anything happening to Kaitlyn hurt Nick in deep places he'd never experienced before and filled him with a violent urge to smash his fist into the man's nose. Did that mean Nick loved Kaitlyn? He shut the thought down. Now was not the time to be thinking of his emotions. He needed to keep a clear head.

"Tsk, tsk." The smug expression on Harrison's face

soured Nick's stomach. "We all know she's the protector. Not you."

Nick wanted to show Harrison just how wrong he was, but decided giving in to his anger wouldn't be a smart move. Better to get as much information out of Harrison as possible, then figure out an escape plan for him and Kaitlyn.

"I'll pilot the plane if you tell me what I want to know," Nick said.

Kaitlyn stared at him. "No."

Giving Kaitlyn a pointed look, Nick said, "Yes."

"I hate to interrupt this little lovers' spat, but we need to go. If you get the plane in the air, I'll gladly answer all your questions, not that it's going to matter."

Nick didn't miss the implication. They wouldn't be alive to do anything with any information he might share. But they were alive now and he would figure out a way for them to survive.

"And make no mistake, Mr. Delaney—you alert the authorities in any way, your girlfriend here will die a slow and painful death," Harrison added.

Stomach curdling from the threat, Nick forced himself to stand, though not fully, to avoid scraping his head on the ceiling.

He stepped into the short aisle and put a hand on Kaitlyn's shoulder. "Don't worry," he said. "Trust me. I've got this." For Kaitlyn and for Rosie.

A myriad of emotions bounced across her face. Worry, regret, anger and something that sent his heart rate soaring. He was afraid to label her look. Better to hold it close until he could ask her exactly what she was feeling toward him. If they managed to live long enough.

He walked into the cockpit and prayed as he'd never prayed before. *Lord, we need You here, right now!*

Trust Nick? Kaitlyn didn't even have to think twice about it. She did trust him. She wasn't sure when she'd begun to think of him as a capable protector. When she'd seen the fierce look of protectiveness on his face when he looked at Rosie? When he'd vowed to keep her safe? Regardless, her opinion of him had definitely changed over the past few days. She no longer considered him irresponsible or superficial. He'd proved time and time again he was the opposite. Her heart fluttered with emotions she didn't have time to examine.

Nick was a pilot, too, like his brother, Ian.

Wow. Never would she have guessed. She'd assumed there would be a hired pilot to fly them to DC.

She watched as Nick took a seat in the pilot's chair. The man was full of surprises. Why was it she discovered astonishing information about Nick at the most inopportune times?

Reece's henchman closed the plane's cabin door and Nick fired up the engine. Kaitlyn put on her seat belt, making sure it was tight and fastened well.

The thug sat in the seat Nick had vacated. He had a clear line of sight to Nick within the cockpit and to Kaitlyn. He held his weapon on his lap, the barrel aimed at her.

She narrowed her gaze at him. "Why are you doing this? You know he'll dispose of you the minute you are no longer useful."

"Frank, don't listen to her," Harrison said. "Deputy, I suggest you be quiet or I'll have Frank tape your mouth closed."

Frank smiled with relish, as if the idea of manhandling her appealed to him. "You grazed my arm. I told you in the hospital you'd pay."

Yes, he had, but she hadn't given it much thought. All law enforcement officers were trained to expect such threats from those on the wrong side of the law. And though Bristle Township was small, she'd encountered a few unruly tourists over the years who'd vowed to get even when she'd hauled them in for some offense or other. Though the first time she'd been verbally threatened had been by Jason, her former college boyfriend, when she'd refused his advances. And he'd gotten even, as he'd said he would.

She sent a prayer that this thug wouldn't be allowed to exact his revenge. And that God would give her the strength to overcome the sense of powerlessness poking at her, trying to shake her confidence.

The plane eased out of the hangar. She twisted around so she could watch Nick. He put on a headset and was doing things with the gauges and the instruments. His voice was loud and clear as he gave the call sign for the plane, telling the control tower they were taking off.

Nick glanced back and met her gaze. He gave her a short nod and turned forward, his focus on getting them off the ground.

Kaitlyn's hands gripped the armrests of her seat. She didn't like flying. She'd only flown once in her life. That was when her family had gone to Oregon and then driven out to the coast. The commercial jet ride had been bumpy, and she'd suffered motion sickness. She prayed she didn't get sick today. That would just make things worse.

They were all silent as the plane taxied out onto the runway. The engines roared with the uptick in speed. She tightened her hold on the armrests. The plane shot forward, the nose of the aircraft lifting toward the sky. Kaitlyn braced herself, pushing backward in her seat to counter the force of the plane climbing in altitude. The sensation of lifting off was bad enough facing forward. Facing the back of the plane was horrible. It took all her strength to keep herself from doing a face-plant into the little table separating her from Reece. The seat belt strap dug in, driving the radio hooked to her belt loop beneath her jacket into her hip. Thankfully, the thug hadn't searched her when she'd entered the plane. Kaitlyn's fingers tingled with the urge to grab the radio and alert Alex to what was going on, but Harrison's hard gaze was steady on her. She'd have to figure out a way to activate the device without the egocentric maniac noticing.

Once they were in the sky, the plane leveled off.

"Give him the coordinates," Harrison said to Frank.

Frank nodded, unbuckled and headed to the cockpit. He handed Nick a piece of paper, then settled into the copilot's seat.

"Where are we going?" Kaitlyn asked as she peeled her hands from the armrests. She shoved them into her pockets and tried surreptitiously to maneuver the radio dial. She didn't know if the frequency would interfere with the plane's technology, but at this point, what choice did she have? She couldn't quite manage to grip the small dial. Noticing Harrison's sharp gaze, she stilled and clenched her teeth in frustration.

"Does it matter?" Harrison replied.

She supposed it didn't. One way or another, she had to figure out a way for the two of them to survive this ordeal. They had so much waiting for them. Little Rosie. Kaitlyn's parents, her fellow deputies, who were like family, and her friends. And whatever it was that was developing between her and Nick. Did she want a chance to explore these uncomfortable yet thrilling emotions gathering inside of her? Maybe. *Please, God, let us get out of this.*

After a few minutes of flying, there was a subtle shift in the trajectory of the plane. Then they were banking. Kaitlyn could only guess they were heading north to Canada.

Harrison held out his hand. "The flash drive."

She tightened her fist around the device in her jacket pocket.

Harrison raised his gun. "Hand it over."

Her heart jumped in her throat. The 9 mm round in his Glock could potentially pass through her body and out the side of the plane. She wasn't exactly sure what would happen, but she imagined it would be bad. "Are you really willing to risk a stray bullet in an aircraft?" she asked. "We could go down."

"I'm an expert marksman," he said. "I don't miss."

Kaitlyn wasn't sure she believed him. If he shot her, even if she managed to survive the wound, firing a round inside the small aircraft would definitely cause damage and put Nick's life at risk. She couldn't do that to him. Rosie needed Nick alive. And Kaitlyn needed to stay focused on an escape plan. She wouldn't take any chances that might prevent Nick and herself from making it out of this ordeal alive. The sheriff's department had a copy of the evidence that would incriminate Reece and Holtsen Pharmaceuticals in the selling of tainted drugs. She would have to be content with that. She slid the flash drive across the table to him.

He pocketed the device. "I assume your sheriff's department made a copy. But you'll never crack this code. It's something of my own design."

Anger and frustration rippled through Kaitlyn. She didn't know how they were going to get out of this situation. She shifted in the seat. The two-way handheld radio poked her in the side again. The radio was their only hope. She crossed her arms over her chest, shoving one hand inside her jacket, trying not to look too obvious as she reached for the radio.

Needing to distract Harrison, she said, "Tell me about Lexi. Why did you have her killed?"

"I didn't want her dead," Harrison said. "My men—" he flicked a disparaging glance at his bodyguard seated next to Nick "—were overzealous in their pursuit. I just wanted her and the flash drive back. I actually loved her."

Her fingers grasped the dial, but she hesitated. What if the radio crackled as it did sometimes?

She needed a cover noise. The only idea she had was to cough. Taking in air, she forced out a coughing fit as she twisted the dial.

Harrison frowned with clear distaste. "Are you sick?"

Grateful there wasn't any static noise from the radio, she cleared her now dry throat. "No. Just thirsty. Being in an airplane with a gunman can do that to a person."

"There are water bottles in the storage compartment," Nick called back. "There's a small hatch between the back seats."

Harrison waved the gun. "Go ahead, Deputy. We'd all like some water."

Hoping the channel on the radio was transmitting, she removed her hand from inside her jacket and undid her seat belt. She found the hatch and lifted the lid. Inside was a cold storage cavity with several bottles of sparkling and still water. She glanced at Harrison, estimating the distance between them to be less than a foot. Could she disarm him without alerting Frank?

Crouched on the floor, she asked, "Are you Rosie's father?"

"No. She did try to pass the baby off as mine, though." He let out a short laugh. "I can't have children, so that was a nonstarter. But I would have still taken care of Lexi and her child. I would have set them up nicely. But I would've never married Lexi. I think that's what sent her running to the FBI."

"If you're not Rosie's father, then who is?" Nick glanced over his shoulder to ask.

Harrison waved a dismissive hand. "Unfortunately, the information may have died with Lexi."

"We know about the tainted drugs," Kaitlyn said, rocking back on her heels. "Holtsen's going down and you with it."

Harrison shrugged. "Holtsen fired me. Whatever they do now is on them."

"Without the pharmaceutical company backing you, how can you afford to pay your men and disappear?" Nick asked.

"Oh, I've been siphoning money off the company for years," he said.

Nausea rolled in her tummy. He was telling them incriminating information that he would never have shared if he planned to let them live. Tension constricted her chest. She pulled in a breath and met Nick's grim gaze. He, too, must have realized Harrison's intent to get rid of them when their usefulness was over.

"Kaitlyn, I'll take a sparkling water," Nick said.

"Me, too," said Frank. He twisted to face them.

They needed to do something sooner rather than later. She didn't have her sidearm, but Nick had a Taser hidden beneath his coat. If he took out Frank, then Kaitlyn could disarm Harrison. Keeping her gaze locked on Nick, she said, "Remember what I gave you earlier? It would be really useful about now, right?"

For a moment, a puzzled expression drew Nick's brows together. Then the frown cleared and his eyes lit up as her meaning dawned on him. "I do. Thank you for reminding me."

"What are you two talking about?" Harrison demanded.

"Nothing," Kaitlyn muttered and grabbed two bottles of water.

"When we land in Canada, then what?" Nick asked as he swiveled the chair to fully face them.

"Hey." Harrison gestured to Nick. "Turn back around and fly this plane."

"It's on autopilot," Nick replied. "Answer my question."

Kaitlyn was grateful for the distraction as she moved closer to Harrison.

"I have another plane waiting," Harrison answered.

Even closer now, Kaitlyn stated, "You'll be a wanted man."

"Not your concern, Deputy. Back in your seat."

Half turning toward the front of the plane, she met Frank's narrow-eyed gaze. "Catch." She flung the bottle of water at him. He fumbled to grab it.

"Now!" she yelled and spun to face Harrison, praying Nick understood what she needed from him. She wrapped her hands around Harrison's gun hand and slid her finger behind the trigger.

She heard the clicking of electricity as Nick deployed the Taser she'd handed him before they rode up the mountain. A loud string of curses emerged from Frank. Then there was a thump as Frank went down.

Kaitlyn wrested the gun from Harrison's hand. She turned to see Nick sitting on Frank's back and tying Frank's hands together with a cord.

She crouched down to look for her sidearm, but it was nowhere in sight. Dread gripped her. She jerked upright just as Harrison pressed the hard barrel of her gun against the side of her head.

"That's enough," Harrison said. He looked at Nick. "What are you doing? Get back at the controls."

Nick raised his hands. Panic darkened his eyes. "Okay, okay."

Kaitlyn had one last opportunity to disarm Harrison. Still in a crouch, she pounced on him, her left arm knocking the hand holding the gun away, and then she struck with her right hand, hitting him in the nose.

He fired a wild shot.

Heart seizing with horror, she turned. "Nick!"

He'd dropped to the floor.

The bullet had lodged itself in the instrument panel. Sparks flew. The engine sputtered and the plane jolted.

Using Harrison's surprise, Kaitlyn grabbed his gun hand and twisted until he let go. Then she shoved him into his seat. She always kept zip ties in the inside pocket of her jacket, and she quickly fished one out. She tied his hands together, then pulled the flash drive out of his pocket.

Trying not to let fear overwhelm her, she stepped over

Frank and moved behind Nick to help him to his feet. "Please, tell me you can get this plane on the ground in one piece."

He sat back in the pilot's seat and put on the head-phones. "Taking over manual control," he said. "The instrument panel's out and so is the communication system. We're going to drop out of these clouds. We need to pray we don't go nose first into a mountain."

Her heart leaped into her throat. "Barring that, you can land without the control panel, right?"

"I've done it in the simulator," he said.

Kaitlyn's heart sank. "That's not quite the same, Nick."

"I understand that, Kait. You hovering is not helping."

"What can I do?"

"Get everyone strapped in," he said. "I'm going to deploy the CAPS."

"The what?"

"The Cirrus Airframe Parachute System." He pointed to a lever with a red handle in the roof over his head. "We're dropping fast. Hurry!"

Panic revved through her veins. She hustled Frank to the back seat next to Harrison. "Strap up," she said. "Let's pray we make it through this alive."

Harrison's lips twisted. "I don't pray."

"I do," Frank said. He bowed his head and clasped his hands.

Kaitlyn stared at him in surprise. Okay. She would not judge. That was for the Lord.

She moved to sit in the copilot's chair and put the seat belt on. "Now what?"

"Everyone sit upright and brace yourself for impact."

Nick reached overhead and pulled the red lever recessed into the ceiling of the cockpit.

A loud explosion rocked through the plane. The world went topsy-turvy, and Kaitlyn held on for dear life as the plane went down.

THIRTEEN

Kaitlyn moaned. The sound reverberated painfully all the way through her body. Or maybe it was just the jarring aftereffects of the crash. Her head hurt and her stomach rolled. Taking stock, she was still belted into her seat in the cockpit of Nick's aircraft. After the explosion that had been set off when Nick pulled the lever over his head, there had been a cacophony of noise and the whole plane had jerked and shuddered. Then it began to drop in a swinging pendulum motion. She closed her eyes tight and prayed for all she was worth, prayed that they survived the fall.

It couldn't have been more than a minute or two before the air was rent with the sound of snapping metal and breaking trees. The plane stopped moving in a shuddering impact with the ground beneath them. At least, she hoped it was the ground and that they weren't hanging in a tree, about to drop again. She ventured to open her eyes. There was a tree right outside the crumpled nose of the plane. An evergreen branch protruded a foot through the window into the space between her and Nick, allowing cold air to blow across her face.

Nick!

Slowly, she turned her head. The movement hurt, her muscles protested and her brain throbbed. She pushed through the pain to look at Nick. His body was upright, his eyes closed.

Please, Lord, please don't let him be dead.

Every cell in her body braced. She didn't know what she would do if he had died in this crash. She'd put him in danger. It was her job to keep him safe. She'd failed. He had to be alive.

A little voice inside her head whispered, *Why is it so important to you, Kaitlyn?*

She pushed the voice aside, unwilling to search her heart for the answer.

His mouth was moving with silent words. Relief, swift and powerful, cascaded through her. He was alive. Whether he was injured or not, she couldn't tell yet. But at least he was alive.

Slowly, she twisted to gaze at the men strapped to the seats in the back, her body protesting as she tried to assess how Harrison and Frank had fared.

Frank was slumped forward, his head between his knees.

Harrison, on the other hand, stared straight ahead, his eyes wide, his pupils dilated. He had a death grip on the arms of the seat and all the color had been leached from his skin, so it matched the color of the salt in his hair. Shock, no doubt.

They all had just suffered a dramatic and horrible experience. But they'd lived through it by the grace of God.

She turned her gaze back to Nick. "Nick." Her voice come out raspy. With a deeper breath, she tried again, stronger this time. "Nick!"

He opened his eyes and looked at her with concern etched on his handsome face. "Are you okay?"

She couldn't help the smile that curved her lips. That was so like him, to be asking about her first, before anything else. He was such a giving and caring man. Why had she never seen the sincere depths of his nature until recently?

"I'm okay," she said. "At least, I think so. We'll know when I try to stand. What about you?"

He wiggled in his seat, rounded his shoulders, flexed his feet. "No worse for the wear, I think." He hitched his chin over his shoulder. "What about them?"

"In shock," she said. "Frank might've passed out."

"No," Frank said. "Just nauseous. Trying not to throw up."

She looked back at Frank. He had straightened and covered his mouth with his hand. Then he bent forward again, putting his head between his knees. Harrison hadn't moved a muscle.

She hoped the shock and adrenaline hadn't given the man a heart attack.

"Can you tell if we're on solid ground or hung up in a tree?" Kaitlyn stretched her neck to look out the window, but the seat belt kept her in place.

"Gauging by the thickness of the tree trunk in front of us, I'm going to say we're near the base of the tree," Nick said. "But there's only one way to know for sure." He undid his seat belt.

"Be careful," she warned, bracing herself in case the plane took another dive.

He half stood to peer out the side window. "I see the ground."

A measure of tension eased from her. "We need to call for help."

"Doubtful there's cell reception in the woods of northern Montana," Nick said. "The emergency system on the plane sent out a distress signal the second it deployed the parachute and has a locator beacon. We'll be found. Eventually."

"How do you know we're in Montana?" she asked. "Where were we when the plane went down?"

"I'd engaged the autopilot because I was busy subduing the copilot." His gaze shot to Frank, who sat shivering beside Harrison. Nick shook his head and continued. "At that point we were flying over Montana, heading for the Calgary airport."

"Unlikely anyone will find us before we freeze in this forest," she said with a sense of doom sinking through her and landing with a hard thud.

Nick's lips pressed together for a second. "What about your radio?"

She nodded. "I may be able to get a signal. But I don't know. I may have to try to find higher elevation, away from the trees."

With hands that shook, she undid her buckle. The seat belt retracted and she was able to take a full breath. Slowly, she moved her feet, her legs and torso to the side. "It's a marvel that we're alive."

Nick shifted in his seat to face her. Their knees touched. He grasped her hands over the branch separating them. "Yes," he said. "Praise God for the airframe parachute system. If we hadn't had that—" He shuddered.

She squeezed his hands. "We did survive. You knew what to do."

"I've taken the training. Twice," he said.

"Twice?" Was he an overachiever, as well?

"The extra time for good measure. As it turns out, though, the training was mostly to mentally and emotionally prepare the pilot to pull the lever. We can't control the plane when there's no way to control it."

She nodded in understanding. "We can always trust that God is in control."

He smiled. "Yes. With God, all things are possible. Even love."

"I suppose you're right."

"I am right," Nick said. "Kaitlyn, I have feelings for you. I'm falling—"

Stunned by his words, she withdrew her hands, cutting him off. "Don't say that. Not now. You can't... I can't."

Her heart stuttered and her emotions flailed. She wasn't sure what she felt for Nick. Was it love? She couldn't process anything right at the moment. Certainly not something so important, so monumental, so life changing as love.

"Don't worry, Kaitlyn. I would never ask more of you than you're willing to give."

Needing to regain her emotional control, she redirected their focus back to their circumstances. Safer that way. She couldn't deal with his declaration. Nor did she believe he really loved her. It was the trauma of being kidnapped and then crashing. It couldn't be real. "You kept your cool in a hairy situation. The training worked."

The corners of his lips lifted, but the smile didn't reach his sad eyes. "Yes, it did. Let's work on getting rescued. We have a mission to complete so we can get back home."

He scooted out of his seat and opened the plane's door. Then he let down the little flight of stairs and left the plane. A cold push of icy air swirled through the plane, making Kaitlyn shiver. She didn't like hurting him. That wasn't her intention. She remained where she was, trying to calm the quaking inside of her. The idea of loving Nick seemed to echo through her heart and her mind.

Giving herself a mental shake to clear her head and center her attention on doing her job, she hustled to Harrison's side. She checked his pulse. It beat rapidly beneath her fingers. She shook him gently. "Harrison," she said. "Can you hear me?"

His eyes focused on her face and he blinked. "What happened?"

"We crashed through the trees," she said. "But we're all alive."

He reached forward and clutched the lapels of her jacket with his zip-tied hands. "Where are we?"

"I don't know." She gripped his wrists and pried his fingers off of her. "And you're still under arrest."

She turned to Frank, who was staring at her warily. He held up his bound hands. "I know, I know. I'm under arrest. You'll get no quarrel from me. God saved my life. All of our lives. I'm turning over a new leaf."

Kaitlyn almost snorted her disbelief. But who was she to quarrel with him?

Kaitlyn hesitated for a moment. Yes, he was a criminal. He'd done bad things. Whether his declaration of redemption was true or not, she needed to make a decision. Should she trust this man?

Her natural inclination was not to, but at the moment, she needed his help getting Harrison out of the plane.

"If you promise me that you won't try to escape or do anything to harm us, I'll allow you to keep your hands free for now." She tapped on the butt of her holstered sidearm. "But don't forget I have a gun."

"Yes, ma'am," Frank said.

She cut his ties, releasing his hands. She'd be wise to stay alert and be cautious around Frank. "Help me with your boss."

They each took a side of Harrison, raising him from his seat. He still seemed to be in shock, his body rubbery, as they maneuvered him to the door of the jet.

Her gaze scanned the snow-covered terrain. The plane had landed in the middle of a forest at the base of a large mountain that looked prime for an avalanche. Nick was standing a few feet away.

"Nick," she called to him. "A little help, please."

He jogged over and stayed her with a raised hand. "Hold up a second." He gave Frank an assessing look. "Shouldn't he be restrained?"

"I needed his help," she told him. "Let's get Harrison over to that fallen tree."

With a frown, Nick nodded. "Fine." Though his tone said it was anything but, and she understood. With the three of them, they were able to get Harrison onto the ground and seated on a nearby downed tree trunk.

She stamped her feet, so grateful to be on solid earth, even if it was covered in icy snow. The chilled air seeped beneath the hem of her jacket. "How much damage has the plane sustained?" She didn't want to be near it if there was a fuel leak.

"There's the tree in the flight deck, some crumpling of the body, but otherwise, it's in pretty good shape, considering we crash-landed through the trees." Nick climbed back into the plane and reappeared a moment later with the black bag Frank had stuffed their cell phones into.

He dropped it on the ground and unzipped it to grab his phone.

"No bars," he said.

She turned to Frank. "Keep an eye on him. He's in shock still. Holler if he passes out." She patted her side-arm as a reminder for him not to try anything before she walked over to Nick. "Is there an emergency kit in the plane? Blankets?"

He tucked his phone into the pocket of his jacket. "Yes, to both. I'll be right back." He headed into the plane.

She noticed that the landing wheels were crumpled beneath the body of the aircraft. A large red-and-white parachute lay tangled in the branches of the trees surrounding them. Long, thick ropes kept the chute attached to the plane.

Nick appeared a few moments later with four silver Mylar thermal waterproof blankets. He put one around Harrison and handed one to Frank. Then he handed one to Kaitlyn, drawing her out of earshot of the other two men.

Nick looked up at the dark clouds gathering overhead. "Doesn't look good," he said in a low voice. "I think we're in for more snow."

A shiver of dread coursed through her. Not what she wanted to hear or even contemplate. How would they make it during a snowstorm? She hurried to try her cell phone and also found no service bars. She tried her radio and encountered only static.

"I need to walk toward civilization."

Nick arched an eyebrow at her. "Which way would that be, Kaitlyn?"

Opening the compass app on her phone, she held the

phone flat. Pointing at the mountain, she said, "That's north."

"Okay, that's helpful," he said dryly. "Nothing notable in that direction. Only three possible ways to go for help. Unfortunately, we have no idea where the nearest town or sign of human life might be."

She hated that he was right. "In the meantime, we could freeze to death." Her gaze landed on his loafer-clad feet. He had to be numb by now, but he wasn't complaining or even showing any signs of noticing the icy temperature.

"There is that," he said. He held out his hand. "Give me your radio. I'll head up the mountain. Maybe with higher ground I can find a radio signal. Or maybe my cell phone will work."

"No. That's ridiculous. You aren't dressed for it and the rescue will come to us, right?" The thought of him going alone was unacceptable, but she realized he'd do it even if it endangered his life. He could get lost. Or fall and hurt himself. He could get eaten by bears. She didn't have any bear spray with her.

Of course, she had her weapon, but hitting a charging bear in the exact spot that would stop the creature would be a million-to-one shot. She was good, but she didn't want to test her skills and fail. She hadn't expected to crash-land in the middle of an unfamiliar forest miles from civilization. If she had anticipated what would happen, she'd have planned accordingly.

Unfortunately, she couldn't predict the future and hadn't had any warning of what was to come. But it was her responsibility to make sure Nick, Harrison and Frank survived.

"Then we need to come up with a plan," he said. "Because Rosie is counting on us to return to her."

A pang hit Kaitlyn in the heart. They had to survive for Rosie. The baby had already lost her mother. It would be a tragedy for her to lose the man who loved her like she was his own. Calling upon her wilderness training, she said, "We need to make a bonfire. Something that will send up a lot of smoke. And then pray someone sees it and points the rescue party in the right direction."

A slow, pleased smile spread over Nick's handsome face. "Good idea, Kait. You're one smart, capable woman." He touched her cheek. "Of all the people in all the world to crash-land in the woods with, I'm beyond glad it was with you."

And he touched his lips to hers, lighting a fire deep within that threatened to consume her. And she had no inclination to douse the flames.

Every cell in Nick's body came to life as his lips touched Kaitlyn's. So soft, so warm, so right. It was as if suddenly a light had been turned on, like the sun had broken through the clouds. He'd never been one for poetry, but sonnets from his college English days filtered through his mind. Words of love, family and hope.

Kaitlyn was part of his family, just as Rosie now was his family. He couldn't see a future where the two of them weren't included.

He ignored the strident voice inside his head that said he couldn't count on love. She'd already rejected his admission that he was falling for her, but in this moment, he wanted to believe they could be a couple, and believe they could make a family with Rosie.

He didn't regret revealing he had feelings for her.

Though he hadn't made the conscious decision to do so. The words had come out of their own volition, surprising him as well as her. But the truth wouldn't be denied. He was falling hard for this woman.

He deepened the kiss. Astonishingly, she kissed him back. Her lips gave and took in a rhythm that made him feel as if they were floating through time and space. He made a low noise of approval in his throat. It seemed to startle her. She stilled, then jerked away from him, her breathing fast. Their gazes locked. She appeared stunned, confused, conflicted.

He reached for her to reassure her, to soothe away the obvious upset taking root and showing in her expression.

She stepped back. "What did you just do?"

He frowned, confusion seeping in. "That would be called a kiss, Kaitlyn."

She touched her lips. "You said you would never do anything to intentionally hurt me."

His breath caught in his lungs, sharp and tight. Hurt her? Never. "I'm sorry, Kaitlyn. I didn't mean— It didn't mean… I'm overwhelmed from the crash and everything."

And he was. His emotions felt out of control, like a plane falling from the sky without a parachute to save the day, and there was nothing he could do to stop the inevitable disaster. He just was so glad they were alive, that she was alive. He didn't think he'd have been able to take it if something had happened to her.

Now his kiss had hurt her. How much clearer could she be that she didn't reciprocate his feelings?

He needed to find a way to get them out of the woods and home. He had to get back to Rosie and her unconditional love. Because apparently any thoughts of him and Kaitlyn forming a future together would only be in his imagination.

Unfortunately, he knew deep in his heart that he could love this woman. What an idiot he was for allowing himself to entertain such an unrealistic thing. Falling in love with the deputy would be a mistake.

She'd said not to talk about his feelings. Clearly, her way of telling him she'd never be open to loving him. She barely respected him. How could he expect her to love him? He couldn't.

That was fine. He didn't need her love or affection. He was good at erecting a barrier around his heart. This time would be no different. He gave a sharp nod of his head to put a period on his own thoughts. "Again, I'm sorry." He stepped away briskly. "Let's build a bonfire."

In silence, they gathered wood. Kaitlyn had employed Frank to help them. Nick wasn't convinced the man wouldn't try to run or something, so he kept a vigilant eye on Frank as they scoured the area for kindling and larger suitable firewood.

Kaitlyn layered kindling pieces of wood between two short, thick logs. She repeated this process until she had three layers. Then she took taller sticks and leaned them against the pile of wood in a tepee configuration, leaving a space.

"You wouldn't happen to have a lighter on the plane, would you?"

Grateful to be of assistance, he said, "Indeed, I do."

She frowned and stared at him like he'd eaten a bug. "Why?"

She was not going to like the answer. But he told her anyway. "In case I want to create some ambience with candles."

She rolled her eyes. "Seriously, you would have a lit candle on a plane?"

He barked out a laugh. "Of course not. But I've been known to fly to places where there are really good picnic spots. In fact, I had the resort put a stocked picnic basket in the storage trunk." He moved to the plane, thankful the area of the fuselage was intact. The door was crumpled and it took effort to get into the compartment. A large picnic basket was strapped to the side of the plane. He unhooked it and brought his bounty out.

"You think of everything, don't you?" There was a hint of aggravation in her tone that he'd heard numerous times before this whole ordeal had begun.

"I do try," he quipped, easily falling back on his flirtatious, deflecting mode, knowing quite well he would put her on the defensive and put them both back on familiar ground. "I was hoping maybe once we finished with our mission in DC, we might then have had a little romantic picnic."

"Did you really."

Keeping his gaze from hers—he didn't want to see her disapproval—he lifted the lid of the basket and fished around inside. "Here's the lighter." He held it out.

She took the device. "Thank you."

He also brought out two boxes of crackers, packages of cheese and assorted meats. "We'll have to ration these. Let's pray it's not too long before we're found."

He gave some of the food supplies to Harrison and Frank, then offered some to Kaitlyn.

She shook her head. "Not yet."

The first flakes of snow started to fall. His prediction had come true. The situation had worsened. He just prayed it didn't become dire.

But he couldn't do anything about the damage to his heart.

FOURTEEN

Fluffy white snowflakes fell from the sky and landed on Kaitlyn's hair and shoulders, stinging her cheeks. Yet she was burning up from the inside as she stood in front of the wood structure she'd created in order to start a fire.

Her mind reeled. Nick had kissed her. More important, she'd kissed him back.

There been no hesitation, no thought of retreat. At least, not at first.

The sensations that rocketed through her at the touch of his lips had been stunning and exquisitely pleasurable, until something inside her brain kicked in, clamoring, *No, no, no. The last time you allowed someone to get this close to you, he hurt and betrayed you.*

She touched her fingers to her lips to keep from screaming, "Nick isn't like that. He would never hurt or betray me."

But did she really know that? He said he loved her. Could she trust his feelings?

"Better get the fire started," Nick said, drawing her focus. "Before the snow turns into more than just a flurry."

Giving herself a little shake, she flipped the switch

on the lighter and a blue flame appeared at the end. Sticking her hand through the opening she'd left in the stacked kindling, she held the flame to the grass and leaves. But they were too wet to ignite. Frustrated, she turned to Nick and froze when she saw the look on his face. Gone was the easygoing, supremely confident expression he normally wore. Instead he appeared...sad? No, not quite. But close enough to be disconcerting. She had to compartmentalize her reactions and emotions. The priority was to stay alive and be rescued. "I need some cardboard or paper to catch the flame."

Seeming to snap out of his mental reverie, Nick nodded and headed back to the plane. She watched him with her heart aching. He'd talked of love earlier, going so far as to say he loved her, and she'd been struck with fear again. That seemed to be a recurring theme for her lately. She'd thought she'd dealt with her issues of fear a long time ago.

While attending the police academy, going through training and being on the job, she'd faced fear every day. Gunmen, bombs, fires and car accidents, not to mention her ex-boyfriend sabotaging her and getting her fired from her college job. But none of her previous experiences came close to what she was feeling now.

Nick had ignited within her a strange and unsettling type of fear. One she was struggling to control.

The subject of her thoughts returned a moment later with the empty cardboard boxes from the crackers, broken down and torn into small pieces. She appreciated that he'd anticipated her next request. She took the pieces and stuffed them in various places throughout the bonfire structure. And then she systematically lit the cardboard on fire. Slowly, flames started to spread until there was enough of a blaze that the foliage caught fire. The long sticks grabbed the flames, sending dark plumes of smoke high into the air. She fanned the smoke, hoping to create enough of the black cloud that someone in the nearest house or town would see the plume and send someone to investigate. It wasn't that she didn't trust the plane's emergency system, but if she could help the search team pinpoint their location, then they'd be rescued that much quicker.

"It's getting colder," Harrison groused from his seat on the downed tree trunk. "What are you going to do now?"

Kaitlyn glanced at Nick and rolled her eyes. "I guess he's come out of his shock."

"Seems like," Nick agreed with the barest hint of a smile. "We should get them back into the plane. In fact, we all should get back into the plane for shelter."

Kaitlyn fanned the steadily growing flames. "I need to stay out here and make sure this fire keeps going."

He glanced upward. "The sun is almost set. I'll get them into the plane. They're not going anywhere. Then I'll come back out here and help you."

She glanced down at his sopping wet pants legs and shoes. Concern arced through her. "You have to be freezing."

He glanced down, his eyebrows rising. "Everything's numb. I hardly feel my feet."

"That's not good," she said. "Let's get you into the plane, as well."

Thankfully her own boots were waterproof. But she wasn't immune to the cold. As if on cue, a shiver rippled through her, intensifying when the sun moved behind the trees, creating long dark shadows.

"I appreciate your concern, Kaitlyn. It's really nice of you," Nick said, his gaze searching her face.

"Don't get used to it," she said without much heat.

He barked out a laugh. "I wouldn't dream of it."

His laughter chased away the chill in a way the blaze she'd started never could. She grinned, then turned away to stoke the fire before she and Nick hustled Frank and Harrison to the plane. Once inside, she got Harrison and Frank situated in the back with their Mylar blankets covering them. Then she turned to Nick, who'd taken a seat in one of the rear-facing leather seats. "Take off your socks and shoes. We need to warm your feet up so you don't lose any toes."

Without comment, he slipped off his loafers, rolled his pants legs up and peeled his dark socks off. With the flashlight from her phone, she assessed his limbs. His skin was icy to the touch and his toes had a bluish tint. She knelt down in front of him and proceeded to rub his feet in an effort to bring some warmth and circulation back into them.

Nick batted at her hands. "Kaitlyn, you don't need to do that."

"Yes, I do. It's my job to protect you. Which includes keeping you from getting frostbite."

Frank snorted. "You can rub *my* feet, Deputy."

She glanced over her shoulder at the man. "Not a chance."

Finally determining Nick's feet were warmed up enough, she wrapped his feet with her blanket.

"You need that blanket," he said.

His concern wrapped her in the kind of warmth a Mylar blanket never could, touching her deeply. He really was a caring man. "I'm going to check on the fire. When

I come back, if your feet are okay, then I'll take my blanket back."

She rose and hopped out of the plane before he could respond. She added more twigs to the growing fire, fanning the plumes of smoke in the hope that, despite the darkening sky, they would be seen.

There was a scuffling noise behind her. Reaching for her sidearm, she turned quickly. Her breath caught in her throat. Nick was wrestling Frank to the ground and Harrison was running into the trees, his silver Mylar blanket flapping behind him like he was some winged creature. In a blink of an eye he disappeared into the darkness.

She gave a shout and started to run after him but stopped. They would both end up lost or worse. The man would return, if he wanted to live. Or maybe he would rather take his chances in the snow than face the reality of a prison sentence. She jogged back to where Nick had Frank pinned to the ground in a choke hold.

Nick grinned and shook his head. "This guy just won't learn."

"You can let him go." She grabbed Frank by the biceps. "I thought you said you were turning over a new leaf."

Frank hung his head for a brief second, then lifted his gaze to meet hers. "Yeah, I'm a work in progress."

"What was the plan?"

"The boss man promised me triple what he was going to pay me if I helped him escape."

"You do realize you both are going to prison," Nick said.

Frank slanted him a glance. "Obviously, you know nothing about the penal system. The dude's got money. He'll have access to it even behind bars. He'll make my life a lot easier with an influx of cash in my commissary account."

Disgusted by the man's thought processes, Kaitlyn pushed him back into the plane and situated in his bucket seat again. Though this time she zip-tied his hands to the armrests so there was no chance he would escape.

She turned to Nick. "Sit down. What were you thinking? You're barefoot."

"I'm aware, Kaitlyn," Nick said dryly, shaking the snow off his feet before taking a seat.

She set to work on warming up his feet again. "You keep putting your life in danger." She couldn't keep the admonishment from her tone. Would the man never learn?

"And you don't?"

"It's my job."

"Maybe I should become a police officer," he said. "I can't see a future where I won't do what's right, even if it means doing something dangerous." He touched her shoulder. "I know you understand."

She did understand. And she really appreciated his honor and integrity. He was nothing like Jason. She'd come to realize that a while ago, but right now, in this moment, the difference had never been clearer. Her heart stuttered. It was time to share her past with him. She wrapped his feet up once again with the blanket, then sat on the floor with her back against the wall so that she could keep an eye on the fire through the side window. She glanced at Frank, wishing there was some way to have privacy. But she wouldn't let the man out of her sight again. And she didn't want to risk Nick getting frostbite by moving them outside so she could be more comfortable telling her story.

"The other night you asked me what had happened to make me so distrusting."

In the moonlight streaming through the front window, Nick's face was bathed in a warm glow. His dark eyes were alert and focused on her. He nodded.

"I'm ready to tell you."

The chill that swept through Nick had nothing to do with the temperature outside or his freezing toes. He was about to hear Kaitlyn's story. He was afraid to breathe in case she changed her mind. He could see the vulnerability shining in her eyes and hear it in her tone of voice. He wanted to take her in his arms, but he sensed that if he moved at all she would shut down. So he kept himself as still as he could, but his body shook and his teeth chattered as the cold seeped into his bones. He really didn't want hypothermia or to miss even one detail of her tale. So he snuggled deeper into the thermal Mylar blanket covering him and willed his body to settle down.

"I was a sophomore in college at the University of Denver. I had a job at the local bakery. It was only part-time but it was great. I mostly worked the front counter and made coffee drinks. I really enjoyed it. Occasionally, I helped out in the back of the house with the prep. The owner of the bakery was a graduate of the university and he liked to employ college students. He and his wife were really good people."

There was a sadness in her voice that made Nick's heart ache. He was touched that she was finally sharing this with him.

"One day this guy, who'd come in a few times before, asked me out. He was handsome and charming. It was very flattering and new. I hadn't had a lot of experience dating. I'd been too focused in high school on my horses and getting good grades. In college, I really wanted to concentrate on graduating at the top of my class."

"You're very competitive," Nick observed quietly. "I actually like that about you."

She tilted her head. "You always know what to say to make me feel better."

He did? That was news to him. But he'd take it. He wanted her to feel good about herself, about life. She was important to him.

"Anyway," Kaitlyn continued. "He asked me out and everybody seemed to like him. The owners knew him and said he was a great guy. I agreed to dinner. He was a real gentleman. So I continued to go out with him. He checked all the boxes. I also discovered he was very affluent and didn't mind letting everyone know."

Nick winced, knowing Kaitlyn couldn't abide braggarts.

"Things were great for a while. But then, as time went on, he became—"

Nick held his breath, waiting. A sense of dread gripped his chest.

"I guess *possessive* is the only way to describe his behavior. He didn't like me spending time with anyone else and would be put out when I would turn down dates with him to study or when I wouldn't skip school or work to be with him."

Nick knew guys like that. Men who wanted to be the sole focus of everyone.

"He arranged with my boss for me to have time off from work. That really upset me. He was messing with my finances. He kept saying not to worry about it. But I did."

"That was very presumptuous on his part," Nick said, not liking this guy at all.

"Yes. He presumed a lot of things. And when I wouldn't take the relationship farther, like he wanted, he grew really nasty."

Nick had a sinking suspicion he knew where this was going. His fingers curled into fists at his side beneath the blanket. "I'm so sorry, Kaitlyn."

She let out a wry laugh. "Don't be. You have to remember, I'm used to bending twelve-hundred-pound beasts to my will. A hundred-and-thirty-eight-pound man was nothing. But I embarrassed him, and he vowed revenge."

Nick's tension eased slightly. "You're a strong, capable woman, Kaitlyn. No one should underestimate you. Ever."

"Again, you have a knack for the right thing to say. I don't understand it. But I do appreciate it."

He was happy to hear her say so. If only that meant she could open her heart to loving him. But he wasn't going to push any boundary she'd set. "What sort of revenge did he exact?"

"He got me fired. Told my boss lies. Said I was skimming product and trash-talking him and his wife. They wouldn't believe me when I denied the accusations. Jason's family had supported the bakery for years. They were one of the bakery's biggest clients. Whenever Jason's family came into town, they would have the bakery cater all their parties. My boss and his wife weren't willing to lose their patronage over me."

"Their loss," Nick stated.

"Sound like idiots to me," Frank piped up.

"Shhhh," Nick hissed at the man.

A small smile curved her lips. "Thanks. Both of you." She sighed. "It was maddening. It made me feel so…"

When she didn't continue, he said, "Small and insignificant?"

"Yes," she said. "I would imagine much the way you felt when you weren't believed as a child."

"True."

"The difference was, I was a grown woman. There was no evidence to support any of Jason's claims. It was very unjust."

"I realized long ago that sometimes justice isn't given here on Earth," Nick stated softly.

"I know one day Jason will have to come to terms with what he's done, and so will my former boss and his wife. I don't wish them ill, but it did leave a mark, as you said."

Now he understood why she'd been so resistant to a relationship with him. To her, he was just another rich boy who thought he could get away with whatever he wanted. He hoped and prayed she had come to realize he wasn't as carefree as he sometimes acted. That his behavior was just his way of keeping the world out. Much the way her icy demeanor and independent stubbornness kept the world at bay for her.

"We're quite a pair," he said. "Both of us trying not to let our guard down or let anybody get too close to us."

"That's true," she said. "It's hard to break down those walls."

"Yes, it is, Kaitlyn. But necessary to let love in."

"I'm not ready for that," she said quietly. "Maybe someday, Nick, but not yet."

She was asking him for time. He understood and really wanted to honor her request, but his heart cried out in despair. Waiting had never been one of his strong suits. Maybe God was trying to teach him patience. And if that was the lesson he was to learn, then he had to just be content with it.

In the meantime, the best he could do was shore up his defenses and concentrate on the love of a little baby who was waiting for him at home. "Kaitlyn, you heard Harrison. He doesn't know who Rosie's father is. Please, tell me you aren't going to look for him."

"Nick, I can't make that promise."

No, the woman who always did the right thing wouldn't promise something she could not deliver.

"The baby's father is not going to be bothering you," Frank interjected.

Nick's gaze zeroed in on the man. "What are you saying?"

"Marcus was the baby's father," Frank said.

"And Marcus is?" Kaitlyn asked.

"The guy who was shot in the hospital," Frank said.

For a moment, Nick was speechless. No wonder the guy had wanted Rosie. And he'd asked about Lexi. He must've cared for her on some level. "Did he know about the fake birth certificate?"

"Yes. They both knew they'd pay if the boss found out about the two of them," Frank said.

In the end, they had both paid the ultimate price. "Is there a real birth certificate?"

Frank shrugged. "Beats me. But I doubt Marcus would have put his name on one."

A noise in the distance, like a low humming, grew closer. The sound was familiar. Nick tilted his head, straining to listen. "Do you hear that? A helicopter."

"Yes!" Kaitlyn scrambled out of the plane. Then she

was running. Nick moved to the doorway. A bright light swept over the area and stopped on Kaitlyn. The helicopter hovered over the crash site. She waved her arms.

From the helicopter, a deep voice rang out clearly. "Deputy Lanz, glad to see you are alive. Search and rescue are on their way."

Nick leaned against the doorjamb. Their rescue had arrived. He was grateful and couldn't wait to get off this mountain. But the future stretched before him in uncertainty. His heart ached, knowing that part of that uncertainty was Kaitlyn. Would she ever let him into her heart?

FIFTEEN

Kaitlyn could barely hear the roar of engines in the distance over the noise of the helicopter hovering above. As the sound drew closer, she recognized the purr of snowmobiles coming in fast. One by one, four search-and-rescue team members arrived on mountain performance motor sleds, forming a half circle around the crash site.

The helicopter flew away, leaving the area dark except for the headlights on the snow machines. Though Kaitlyn had never ridden one of the snowmobiles, she was impressed. Each motor sled was outfitted with two skis in the front and a large traction belt in the back. She was glad to see the machines were fitted with seats for two people. She didn't relish the ride to civilization on a rescue litter.

A woman removed her helmet and got off her machine. "Deputy Lanz?"

"Yes, I'm here," Kaitlyn said as she hurried forward to greet the woman, holding out her hand. "Call me Kaitlyn. Where are we?"

The woman tugged off her glove to grasp Kaitlyn's hand. "Bev DeSalvo." She released Kaitlyn's hand. "Glacier National Forest. About forty miles outside Eureka,

Montana. I apologize we were unable to make it sooner. There was an avalanche on the other side of this mountain that trapped a couple of people. Once that rescue was completed, we had to regroup and restock equipment. Then we followed the locator beacon. We knew we were going the right direction when we saw the plumes of smoke. You're doing okay?"

Grateful to have been found, Kaitlyn said, "Yes, we're good now."

"Well done on the bonfire. We'll douse it before we leave," Bev said with approval. "Do you have any injured?"

"Our pilot might have an issue with his feet." Kaitlyn prayed Nick didn't have frostbite. "We should get him into town for medical attention ASAP. Also, I have a suspect that escaped into the woods."

"We have a medic. Greg!" Bev signaled for one of the riders. "He'll check all of you to be on the safe side. I'll have to send another team out to search for this suspect. We're spread thin right now."

A man climbed off his machine and strode forward with a red medical bag. "What do we have?"

"This way." Kaitlyn directed the man to where Nick sat inside the plane.

Greg tended to Nick's feet. "No frostbite, yet. Good thing we arrived when we did."

Nick held up his soaking socks and shoes. "Any chance you have some dry ones available?"

"Yes, sir," the medic said. "Hang tight." He used his radio to talk to another team member who rushed forward with dry socks and fleece-lined rubber boots.

While Nick put on the footwear, the medic checked on Kaitlyn and Frank, and deemed them unharmed. Kaitlyn released Frank from his seat, then retied his hands together. "Don't try anything," she warned.

He shrugged. "I'm cold and hungry. Right now, even jail sounds good."

She escorted Frank out of the plane. To Bev, she said, "I need to talk to the police chief. This man is under arrest. The suspect who escaped on foot took off about an hour ago."

"I'll radio the chief." Bev waved over another team member. "John can take care of this guy."

A big burly man stepped forward. Kaitlyn handed Frank off, explaining the situation.

"Don't worry, ma'am," John said in a drawl that made her think he was from the South. "He won't get away from me. We're set up for this sort of issue." He took Frank by the arm and led him to his snowmobile, securing him on the back seat by looping a rope through his tied hands and attaching it to a metal ring on the seat. If Frank tried to jump off, he'd be dragged alongside the motorized sled.

"All right, people, let's move." Bev whirled her hand in the air as a signal to move out. To Kaitlyn she said, "You'll ride with me while your friend will ride with Greg."

Nick got on the back of the medic's snowmobile. They were given helmets and goggles and were wrapped in fresh Mylar blankets.

Then they were off, headed toward the search-and-rescue team's headquarters in the town of Eureka, Montana.

A police vehicle and an ambulance, their red and blue lights dancing through the darkness, waited for them in a plowed parking area at the trailhead as the snowmobiles emerged from the forest. They were on the outskirts of a place that reminded Kaitlyn a lot of Bristle Township, quaint with rustic charm. Snow was piled on the rooftops and at the sides of the roads.

Bev introduced Kaitlyn to the police chief. He was a tall, lanky man with dark hair beneath a winter hat. "Chief Warren Kirkland."

"Deputy Lanz." Kaitlyn shook the man's hand. "I have a suspect I need housed until other arrangements can be made, and we have another fugitive on the run somewhere on the mountain."

"We can head to the station." Kirkland gestured toward his vehicle. "I'll coordinate with Bev for a search."

"I'll be right back," she told the chief.

While John and the police chief got Frank settled in the back of the Eureka PD's official SUV, Kaitlyn hurried over to Nick.

"I'm fine," Nick said. "Greg and the paramedics said there won't be lasting effects on my feet. They suggested the Bluebird Hotel down the way."

"Good news," Kaitlyn said. "I'll arrange for you to be taken to the hotel while I get Frank settled in over at the police station. I need to touch base with Alex and let the FBI know about Harrison. I'll see you later at the hotel."

Nick nodded. "Sure. You do what you need to. Don't worry about me." His gaze held hers, his expression serious. "Thank you, Kaitlyn, for everything."

She frowned. That sounded so final. Like he was saying they wouldn't be seeing each other again. Had he decided that he was done with her because she'd put him off without giving the response he wanted to his declaration of love? Surprised and hurt, she mentally took a step back. Of course, Nick was, after all, a wealthy man used to getting his way. Maybe she'd been fooling herself, thinking he wasn't like Jason.

With a sharp nod, she turned away and headed back to the police car. "I'm coming with you to the station, Chief, if you don't mind. I want to make sure Frank gets safely put into a cell. And I need to contact the FBI."

The chief nodded and gestured toward the vehicle. "Come on and let's get going."

The chief took them to the police department, which shared the town's Justice Center with the courthouse and other official public departments. Snow had been shoveled from the sidewalk and piled high on each side.

Somebody had made a snowman, complete with mismatched button eyes and a carrot for a nose. The bit of whimsy made Kaitlyn smile. And it also made her think of Nick. Building a snowman on the Justice Center's lawn seemed like something he would do. She could imagine him out on the expansive backyard of the Delaney estate, rolling large snowballs to make a snowman. One day Rosie would be old enough to help him.

Kaitlyn's heart ached to think she would not witness such a precious scene.

She didn't want to miss that. But if things kept going as they were, she would not be a part of Nick and Rosie's life.

Why?

Because of her pride and stubbornness and fear. All things that were hard to let go of, but she would need to let them go if she hoped to ever have a future that included Nick. She knew in her heart of hearts that Nick was honorable and honest.

As she followed the chief and Frank into the building, she berated herself for holding back in a vain attempt to be better than anyone else by not letting anybody get close. What a sham she was!

She wanted to be part of the family Rosie and Nick made. A swell of certainty and determination engulfed her. She was going to tell Nick what she wanted as soon as she saw him again. But first she needed to do her job.

Once Frank was settled on a cot in the police department's cell, Kaitlyn used the police chief's landline in his office to call Alex, who gave her the number for the special agent in charge at the FBI. She dialed and the agent answered on the first ring.

"I have the flash drive," she said to the man. "You're going to need to come and get it. I'm headed back to Colorado as soon as this storm breaks. Harrison Reece is on the loose. I'm sure he'll head to Canada. He claims to have a plane waiting at the Calgary airport."

"That man is going to be the bane of my existence," he said. "I will send agents to Montana right now to find Reece, and by the time you get back to Bristle Township, I'll have a team waiting to take possession of the flash drive."

Kaitlyn breathed out her relief and hung up, her mind turning back to Nick. She planned now to go to the hotel and talk to him. Would he accept her apology for being so prideful, so fearful?

A commotion in the outer office drew her attention. She left the chief's office to find a young officer leading an older man sporting a head wound. Blood had run down his face and soaked the front of his jacket.

"What's happened, Dave?" Chief Kirkland asked, his nose wrinkling. "You smell like gasoline."

The officer helped the man to sit in a chair in the waiting area.

"I was carjacked, Chief," Dave said. "At the Gas and Go. This guy came out of nowhere. Rammed my head into the side of my truck, then pushed me down and jumped in and took off while the pump was still running."

Kaitlyn's heart jumped in her throat. Anxiety twisted in her chest. "Did you get a look at the man?"

Dave shrugged. "Just briefly. Kind of a big guy, wearing a long fancy coat that was soaked. He didn't look like he was from around here."

"Harrison Reece," Kaitlyn said. "He's going to head for the border."

Chief Kirkland nodded. "I'll contact the state patrol and the county sheriff. For now, Deputy, you've done your duty. It's time for you to go to the hotel and rest."

Kaitlyn knew she had no jurisdiction here, and though she hated to admit it, she was exhausted. But she couldn't leave when there was work to be done. "I should stay and help with the search."

The chief shook his head. "No offense, Deputy, but you were just in a plane crash. You look wrung out. I think the strongest wind could blow you over. You need rest. Let us take over from here. Officer Hess, take Deputy Lanz over to the Bluebird Hotel."

She wanted to protest. Harrison was her responsibility. She'd let him get away. His escape was a mark on her record.

There's that pride and stubbornness again, Kaitlyn, a little voice whispered in her head.

Mentally grimacing, she said, "You're right. Just let me know when you catch him." She started to leave with the young officer when she paused and turned back to Dave. "Please, tell me there are no weapons in your truck."

The man shrugged. "Just my shotgun."

Kaitlyn's stomach dropped. "Harrison's armed and dangerous. No one's safe until he's caught."

"I understand, Deputy. I will make sure everyone uses caution," the chief promised.

"He has nothing to lose," she told him. She stuck her hand in her jacket and fingered the flash drive. Harrison wouldn't dare come after the drive, would he? He'd be a fool if he did. But she'd be ready for him.

The hotel was just a few blocks away. As Officer Hess pulled beneath the porte cochere, he said, "Hey, there's Dave's truck."

"What? Where?" Every cell in Kaitlyn's body went on alert.

Officer Hess pointed to a big silver American-made dually truck.

Terror struck Kaitlyn's heart.

Harrison was here.

And Nick, the man she loved, was vulnerable. She had no doubt Harrison would use Nick as leverage to get the flash drive. It was up to her to protect Nick.

After a long hot shower, Nick dressed in the sweatpants and long-sleeve T-shirt provided by the hotel gift shop. He was warm and dry and famished. He'd called room service before his shower and ordered a juicy hamburger with the works, fries and a bottle of water. He would've ordered Kaitlyn the same, except he didn't know when, or if, she'd be coming to the hotel. And he was sure she wouldn't be coming to see him. Though she'd asked for time, he was certain she'd really meant never.

It hurt to think that she wouldn't ever let him into her heart. But somehow he was going to have to live with her rejection.

He had a child now who would require his attention and his love. That was, if all went the way he hoped and prayed it would when he filed to adopt Rosie. She would love him unconditionally. He'd never had anyone in his life love him for himself. He knew it wouldn't be all smooth sailing, being a parent. He was realistic enough to know he had a lot to learn.

But he was hopeful that he and his little girl would bond, and he would be enough for her. Just him. He couldn't imagine raising her with anyone other than Kaitlyn.

And Kaitlyn had already made it clear she wasn't interested in being a part of their lives.

A knock sounded at the door. "Room service."

Finally. His stomach growled. "Coming."

He padded across the floor in his new socks and opened the door. Harrison Reece stood there with a shotgun aimed at a wide-eyed waiter gripping a rolling cart bearing a silver tray of food.

Nick gulped air as his heart rate took off at a gallop in his chest.

Harrison pushed the waiter inside the room. "Back up, both of you." He dragged the rolling cart in and slammed the door behind him, locking it.

The waiter, probably in his early twenties, was visibly shaken. Nick pushed the young man behind him. "Harrison, what are you doing? You need to let this kid go. He has nothing to do with this."

"Oh, no," Harrison said. "He's my insurance that you'll cooperate."

"Everybody's going to be looking for you. It's only a matter of time before they find you and you go to prison," Nick stated.

Keeping the shotgun level, Harrison shook his head. "You're my ticket out of here. Nobody is going to hurt me as long as I have the great Nick Delaney, son of the eccentric billionaire Patrick Delaney, as my hostage."

"How did you find me?" Nick asked.

"The front desk clerk is a few hundred dollars richer," Harrison said.

"This isn't going to do you any good." Nick's nerves stretched taut. He wanted to do something, anything, to thwart Harrison. But as long as Harrison had that shotgun aimed at him, he couldn't act. He didn't have his flak vest on anymore. He really didn't want to die. He had too much to live for. "The FBI know about you and about the flash drive. They will hunt you down no matter where you go."

"You keep telling yourself that." Wedging the butt of the shotgun against his shoulder, his finger near the trigger, Harrison used his other hand to lift the lid on the service tray and grab the hamburger. "Thank you, Nick. Don't mind if I do." He proceeded to eat the burger.

Nick tried to think of some way to get himself and the waiter out of there. He glanced over his shoulder at the kid and asked softly, "What's your name?"

"Bobby."

"Okay, Bobby. Just don't do anything and stay behind me."

Bobby nodded.

When Harrison was done with the hamburger, he went

to the desk and picked up Nick's phone. He tossed it to Nick. Nick caught it.

"Call the deputy," Harrison said. "Tell her to bring the flash drive here. And to come alone. Make sure she knows I'll put a bullet through you and the kid if she doesn't comply."

Nick had Kaitlyn on speed dial. He pushed the number and it went right to voice mail. "Kaitlyn, listen to me. I need you to bring the flash drive to my room at the hotel, alone, or Harrison says he will put a bullet through me and the waiter who brought my room service dinner." He ended the call. "I don't know if or when she'll get the message."

"Then we wait till she does," Harrison said.

A few seconds later the phone rang in Nick's hand. It was Kaitlyn. Nick pressed the button to connect the call.

"Just listen to me," Kaitlyn said crisply. "When you hear a knock at the room door, use the distraction to unlock the glass slider."

"Okay," he said and hung up. He wasn't sure what was about to happen, but he trusted Kaitlyn and would do as she instructed.

Harrison frowned. "What did she say?"

"She's on her way." It wasn't a lie. He assumed Kaitlyn was close.

"Good." Harrison ate a fry.

There was a knock on the room door. Harrison turned toward the sound.

Adrenaline spiked through Nick. He ran the short distance to the slider and flipped up the lock. Then his gaze focused on the woman standing on the other side of the sliding glass door. Kaitlyn. She must have climbed to the balcony.

"Move away from there!" Harrison yelled.

Nick backed away as Kaitlyn opened the slider and stepped into the room.

Nick grabbed Bobby and yanked him to the floor.

"Drop your weapon, Reece," she said, her voice calm and steady, as was the gun in her hands. "You're under arrest."

"Not on your life, Deputy." Harrison pulled the trigger on the shotgun.

Kaitlyn dived to the side and came up firing.

The sounds of gunfire and glass shattering were followed by an eerie silence.

Kaitlyn!

Nick's heart slammed against his ribs. Had Harrison shot the woman Nick loved?

Nick covered his ringing ears and lifted his head. Harrison lay crumpled on the floor, gripping his shoulder. Blood seeped into the carpet beneath him, creating a wide circle. Nick twisted to look at Kaitlyn. She was on one knee, her weapon still aimed at Harrison. The shotgun blast had hit the sliding glass door leading to the balcony instead of hitting Kaitlyn.

She was okay. Relief flooded Nick.

Kaitlyn rose and grabbed the shotgun, moving it far from Harrison's reach. She turned to Nick, her eyes wide and her pupils dilated. "Are you okay?"

Able to read her lips, he nodded. "Except for the ringing in my ears, yes."

She gave a sharp nod before she opened the hotel room door.

Two officers charged in. Nick recognized the police chief, who assessed Harrison's wounded shoulder and called for an ambulance.

Kaitlyn took Nick's hand and held on tight. "We'll need to give our statements."

Bemused by her action, Nick nodded. "Of course." He squeezed her hand. "You saved my life."

"I did my job, Nick."

But the way she was holding on to him wasn't part of her job. And not for anything would he point that out.

Paramedics arrived to take Harrison to the hospital. The other officer followed them out, reading Harrison his rights. Nick, Bobby and Kaitlyn gave their statements to the police chief.

Once everything settled down, the hotel manager gave Nick a key card for a suite on the top floor.

Fully expecting Kaitlyn to detach, Nick was pleasantly surprised when she kept hold of his hand and entered the elevator to the top floor. In silence, they walked to the suite at the end of the hall. He opened the door to a spacious living room and small kitchen. There was a bedroom off each end of the living room.

Nick flexed his fingers, assuming Kaitlyn would let go, but she didn't. He turned to her. She was so pale. Her pupils were dilated. Tears gathered in her eyes. His strong, beautiful, capable Kaitlyn was on the verge of a breakdown. And she was fighting it for all she was worth.

He led her to the couch and sat down next to her. "It's okay, Kaitlyn. We're safe. Harrison is no longer a threat to any of us." He realized this could be the first time she'd shot someone in the line of duty. "You did what you had to do. To protect me. To protect everyone. That's who you are, Kaitlyn. A protector. And I love you."

Her only response was a little hiccuping noise that

broke his heart. Was she going into shock? "Kaitlyn, you need to let it all out or it's going to eat you up inside."

Her gaze met his. The vulnerability and anguish he saw swimming in her pretty eyes hurt his heart. He tugged her to his chest. For a moment, she resisted. Then she melted against him. He was at a loss for what to do. Love filled him to brimming and he did the only thing he could. He held her through the storm.

Kaitlyn's sobs turned to hiccups until she was able to control them. She felt spent, yet the crying jag had been cathartic. Her cheek lay against Nick's chest. His heart beat in a wild rhythm. His shirt was soaked from her tears. She'd never cried like that before. Embarrassment flashed through her. Then she reminded herself this was Nick. The man she loved. He would never intentionally hurt her. He would not see her as weak.

She lifted her head and leaned back so that she could stare into his handsome, dear face. "Nick, I'm so sorry."

He frowned with clear puzzlement. "What for, Kaitlyn? You have nothing to apologize for."

"But I do," she insisted. "You see, I let my pride and my stubbornness keep me from acknowledging what my heart has known for a very long time. I let fear keep me imprisoned." She took a steadying breath, determined to say the words clearly. "I love you, Nick Delaney."

His mouth formed an O and his eyes widened. She waited, wondering if he would come back with some flippant remark, and she knew she wouldn't mind.

Instead, he smiled, a soft, tender smile that made her heart soar.

He touched her cheek. "Praise God. I'm so glad to hear that."

She needed him to understand. "I want to be with you. If you'll have me."

His eyebrows arched and that impertinent grin she loved so much formed.

"Kaitlyn Lanz, are you proposing to me?"

She laughed as joy bubbled up inside of her. "I suppose I am. I guess you want to be the one to do it, don't you?"

"Well, traditionally the man does the proposing. But I kind of like that you're taking the lead on this." He gave a dramatic sigh. "Though I have to say I was really hoping for something more romantic."

Grinning, she arched her eyebrow. "Really? Like what?"

"Like Paris, the top of the Eiffel Tower, with roses and chocolate-dipped strawberries."

Her heart sighed at the image his words created. "I wouldn't mind that at all. Can we bring Rosie?"

He laughed. "Of course. Providing the court lets me adopt her."

"I'm confident you will become her forever daddy," she said as she pulled him closer.

"And you'll be her forever mommy," he murmured, right before he kissed her.

EPILOGUE

Morning sunlight glittered through the dining room window, making the ornaments on the large Douglas fir tree glisten. Nick sat on the floor with Rosie on his lap, her little hands holding on to his fingers.

It had been two weeks since Rosie had come into Nick's life. After petitioning the court for custody and it being granted, then starting the adoption process, Nick looked forward to the new chapter in his life. Despite the sad circumstance that had brought Rosie to him, he could honestly say his life had changed for the better.

Now it was Christmas morning, and for the first time in his adult life, excitement revved through Nick's veins at the thought of celebrating the blessed day, because this was his first Christmas with Rosie.

And Kaitlyn.

She'd arrived an hour ago with her parents, having declined to stay at the estate, saying she didn't want to give the town gossips any fodder. But soon they would all be flying off to Paris for a proper proposal. Kaitlyn's parents were coming along to help with Rosie. And a wedding was in the works for the spring.

Mr. and Mrs. Lanz were sitting at the table with Margaret and Collin, enjoying the last of a hearty Christmas breakfast.

"Here's a present for you." Kaitlyn handed him a beautifully wrapped gift as she sat beside him. She reached for Rosie. "Let me have a turn."

Marveling yet again at how blessed he was to have this woman in his life, Nick relinquished his hold on Rosie to open the box. Inside was an ornament, an exact replica of his Cirrus jet that had crashed in the mountains of Montana. "This is fabulous. Where did you get it?"

She smiled over Rosie's head. "You can find anything on the internet."

He laughed and hung it on the nearest limb of the Christmas tree. Then he reached under the tree, past the many presents for Rosie, for his gift to Kaitlyn. "I have something for you, too."

Keeping Rosie on her lap with one arm around her tiny waist, Kaitlyn held out her hand.

Nick laughed, content to let her keep Rosie so he could look at them both. He placed the small box in her palm.

She stared at it for a moment, then lifted her gaze to his. "Is this—?"

No doubt she wondered if it was the beautiful ring they'd had made by the local jeweler. Nick had wanted to make sure Kaitlyn liked her ring, so he'd had her pick it out. He shook his head. "No, you'll have to wait for that. This is something else I hope you'll like."

She attempted to unwrap it with one hand. He couldn't take it, so he helped. He lifted the lid to reveal the delicate rose-gold snowflake charm on a rose-gold chain.

"I love it," she said. "Will you?" She gestured to her neck.

He removed the necklace and went behind her to secure it around her throat. It rested on her skin above the collar of her Christmas sweater. "Beautiful. Like you."

A noise at the front door jarred them from the moment, sending Nick's pulse skyrocketing. Apparently, it did the same for Kaitlyn. She shoved Rosie into his arms and scrambled to her feet, her hand reaching for a sidearm that wasn't there.

Nick stood. Then his brother, Ian, wheeled their father into the dining room. Nick's knees nearly gave out in relief.

"We made it," Patrick Delaney declared, clearly oblivious to the scare his arrival had caused. "Merry Christmas."

Nick introduced Ian and Patrick to the Lanzes. Margaret and Collin set out plates for the new arrivals.

Kaitlyn sagged against Nick. "At some point we will stop reacting to every noise."

Tucking Rosie against his left side, he snaked his other arm around Kaitlyn. "Yes, we will. But I will never stop loving the people making the noise."

He was grateful to be surrounded by family. It was everything his young heart had dreamed of during his days at boarding school. However, he'd never dared to dream of experiencing the love of a sweet baby like Rosie or a woman as strong and beautiful as Kaitlyn. And now Christmas would forever be his favorite holiday. He was so blessed.

* * * * *

If you enjoyed this story, look for these other thrilling tales from Terri Reed for Love Inspired Suspense:

Secret Mountain Hideout
Buried Mountain Secrets

Dear Reader,

I hope you enjoyed this latest book set in the fictional town of Bristle Township, Colorado, as much as I enjoyed writing it. Pairing Nick and Kaitlyn together came naturally. They had such great chemistry together in the two previous books, *Buried Mountain Secrets* and *Secret Mountain Hideout*, that I had to tell their love story. Nick used humor and flirting as a way to keep an emotional barrier against the world, while Kaitlyn hid her heart behind stubbornness and her job. They both had to come to a point where they were willing to let down their guards and open their hearts to the possibility of love. Throwing in an adorable baby girl seemed like just the catalyst for Nick and Kaitlyn to expose their pasts, heal their wounds and forge a future together. They had many lessons to learn along the way, but in the end, they were able to break down the walls and begin a new journey together as a family.

Stay safe and healthy,
Terri